The
SCREAMER
DOWN THE HALL
and Other Tales

TIM
RITTER

Publishing Coordinator – Sharon Kizziah-Holmes
Cover Design – Jaycee DeLorenzo

Paperback-Press
an imprint of A & S Publishing
Paperback Press, LLC
Springfield, Missouri

ISBN -13: 978-1-964559-92-6

DEDICATION

To the memory of my late brother, Doug, with many thanks for bringing Edgar Allan Poe into my life.

CONTENTS

INTRODUCTION

In 1975, my brother Doug, who collected such magazines as *Mad*, *Cracked*, and *Movie Monsters*, brought home Issue Number 69 of a magazine called *Creepy*, which had been in publication since the month before I was born, November 1964. From a company called Warren Publications, *Creepy* took classic and contemporary spooky stories and adapted them into what the world now calls graphic novels. Issue Number 69 was comprised of six stories written by none other than Edgar Allan Poe. The stories included "The Pit and the Pendulum," "The Oval Portrait," "The Case of M. Valdemar," "Premature Burial," "The Fall of the House of Usher," and "MS. Found in a Bottle." I was spellbound.

Later, at the ripe old age of thirteen, after studying Poe in junior high English class, I decided that I was going to be the next Poe, so why not start right then and there. Our assignment one day was to pick an object in the room and describe it without actually saying what it was. I picked a filing cabinet and decided to impress the girls in the class with my vivid but dark description of the black beast, including the observation that it looked like something that belonged in a morgue. I heard one of the girls sigh, "Good lord," and my teacher paused then said, "That was interesting, Tim. However, I think you may have taken that a bit too far." And she was right. I decided that perhaps I wasn't ready to be the next Poe.

In my adult life, I have studied not only Poe but also one who stated he was inspired by Poe, Ambrose Bierce. I found Bierce to be the master of the surprise ending, along with a rather deadpan, matter-of-fact voice in his writing. Both men, Poe and Bierce, became my literary heroes.

In 2019, as the 170th anniversary of Poe's death came

around, I wanted so badly to write something about his final days or hours. It had to be something unique, written from an angle no one attempted before. So, I began to think about his suffering in the hospital, and the claims of Doctor John Joseph Moran, who said Poe called out the name "Reynolds" repeatedly in his delirium. I decided to explore what it might have been like to be a dying patient down the hall from Poe's room, listening to him yelling repeatedly. After a few iterations, the poem "The Screamer Down the Hall" was born.

After completion of the poem, I learned of a contest that had been created as part of the annual International Poe Fest in Baltimore, Maryland. The contest was called the Saturday Visiter Awards, named after the publication, with the word "Visiter" intentionally misspelled, which was the first to publish one of Poe's works and pay him for it. The awards solicited writings and various other forms of art which were inspired by or related to Poe's writings or pertained to his life. Since it related to his death, I submitted "The Screamer Down the Hall" to the contest and waited, all the while remembering the disgusted sigh of the girl in seventh grade.

One day in the Spring of 2020, I received a large envelope in the mail from the Poe Festival. To my amazement, my poem had been selected a finalist for that year's Visiter Awards. It included a certificate as a finalist, and a letter which noted that my submission was one of the best they had received. I was absolutely thrilled.

Note, however, that it was 2020. Covid had gripped the world, and by the time of the October festival, it was decided that the Visiter Awards ceremony would have to be remote, as so many special events were. I dressed nicely and sat in front of my computer camera through the event. Alas, my poem was not selected as a winner that night. But the fact that it had been selected as a finalist gave me a feeling of validity, that perhaps my work was worth reading. And I decided that I should include the "Screamer" poem in some sort of collection, as a nod to Poe and Bierce to thank them for their inspiration. That collection you now hold in your hand.

I would like to thank my buddy and fellow author John Cawlfield for all the monthly chats over lunch and for being such a great sounding board and mentor. Thanks to Jaycee DeLorenzo for the great cover work, and to Sharon Kizziah-Holmes at Paperback-Press for all her help getting this together. Many thanks to my editing team: Kate Richards, Addison Williams, and Nan Mabbitt. Thanks also to Paul McSorley, the voice of these stories in the audiobook version. Thanks also to Enrica Jang at the Poe Baltimore Museum. Many thanks also to my sisters, Debbie and Kathy, for being brave test readers. And finally, many thanks to my wife Lisa, for her love and support.

THE SCREAMER DOWN THE HALL

Reynolds!
Reynolds!

Oh, how he screams,
That man down the hall -
That poor cursed man,
Wretched man,
Tortured man.
Peace, I know he seeks.
Peace, I know I seek.

Myself,
I am sick, sick nearly to my death.
The fever takes me.
The fever makes me
Swoon.

Yet that man, repeatedly he screams.
How he calls out,
Gasps,
Moans in agony,
Groans in agony,
Adds to my agony.

Reynolds!
Reynolds!

Oh God, again the screams.
His cries fill this, my dank room,
My wretched room,
My wretched tomb.

His cries surround me,
Astound me,
Confound me,
Though his chamber
Be removed from my own
By two,
Just two walls.

Please, Providence, I beg you,
If I deserve any mercy,
Silence the man.
Silence his cries, give him peace.
Silence his cries, give me peace.
If I could but rise, could free myself
Of this ward, crowded,
Filled with the dying,
Filled with the dead,
Filled with the dread;

Upon my rising, my freeing, fleeing,
Past the room next would I *trebucher*
To the bed of the screamer,
He, the dreamer,
A prisoner in his own nightmare.

Yet I know not my *geste*
Upon entering his ward,
Looking down upon his tortured soul;
Writhing as I stare,
Perspiring as I stare,
Dying as I stare.

Gaze silently would I?
Administer aid would I?
Scream "Silence!" repeatedly with no mercy
Till I could no longer speak would I?

Alas...
Here I remain,
Confined to my dread,
Confined to my bed,
Soft as granite,
Cold as granite,
Not unlike the granite that will soon over me reside.

Reynolds!

Again, he screams,
Yet this time but once
The name he calls,
The name he wails,
The name I will not forget...

Welcome Silence to this ward,
Welcome is your return.
Those of us dying,
Those of us dead,
Require silent rest
Before our final Rest.
Rest.
Ressssssssssst...

Suddenly I awaken
As if by the Reaper shaken,
My eyes, they open
And I know not where am I.

But my sight returns
And I take note of the walls
And the granite
Ah, the granite.

In my ward I remain.
Yet the silence,
The pounding, screaming silence
Deafens me
As he who screamed that name
Screams no more.

Doctor Moran enters the room,
Skeletal, muddled, begrimed
From the hazards of his keep,
From the hazards of no sleep.
Inquire must I.

Doctor, who is that man?
The man who wails that name
And shares his horror,
Shares his agony,
With me?
Does he who screams rest now?
Scream again will he
When from his rest he awakens,
When from his rest he returns
To the horror?

"Rest? Yes, rest does he,"
The doctor grimaces,
"The bearer of screams.
Rest does he,
Rest do we.
Screamed his last, has he,
The man of screams,

That man of dreams.
No more that name shall you hear,
No more that name shall we hear."

Tell me then, Doctor,
If gone is he,
Tell me his name,
The man of screams.

The doctor looks down upon me,
A weak smile does his face betray.
"A writer of tales was he, so he claimed.
His name was Poe, Edgar Poe."

Back down upon the cold granite do I lie,
The name of the screamer known.
Nevermore will I hear the shrieks of his terror,
Nevermore will I hear the terror of his shrieks.
But I know well
Evermore will I hear the name

Reynolds...

MIND THE LEG, MADELINE

———————— •●• ————————

Where do the most frightening monsters dwell: under our beds or within our heads?

If you want to live to see tomorrow morning, listen to me. Two unbreakable laws govern the process of retiring for the evening. Period. Following these rules not only ensures restful sleep; attention to these nocturnal requirements absolutely, positively saves your very soul on a nightly basis. Therefore, you must listen to me.

As a child, I obeyed these rules to the letter. I guess such a statement is quite obvious, because had I not followed them, surely I would not be here today, sharing this tale with you. And now, I find it most important, most crucial, to share these guidelines, these rules, these laws with you. I do this out of care for your safety and well-being.

The first rule: Always be certain the door to your closet is closed and latched before crawling into bed. This prevents any specters dwelling within the vestiary from getting out during the night, lest they attack and eat you.

The second rule: Never, under any circumstances, allow your arm, leg, or foot to be exposed while you sleep, and for the love of all things holy, DO NOT let such appendages dangle loosely and carelessly over the side of the bed as you rest in quiet slumber. Otherwise, the beast under your bed could reach up and grab you, then pull you down under the bed, do terrible things to you, and ultimately eat you.

I sense some scoffing, some of the doubting of Thomas, as you listen to my story. But dear friend, I must tell you I have proof of the necessity of these commandments. I am sad to say some individuals familiar to me have not followed these rules, and as a result, they no longer walk among us. Their tales are tragic, and it pains me to think these souls would still be alive had they heeded these simple edicts.

Pertaining to the first rule, I speak of poor old Jules Cauchemer, who lived on Dumaine Street in the heart of the Bayou St. John region of New Orleans. Jules was what one might classify as a bit of a hermit, a loner, having been widowed many years before his demise. Superstitious to a fault, Jules lived a lifetime of trepidation, always careful to avoid the conjuring of evil spirits, or the angering of the benevolent ghosts he was convinced surrounded him within the dark and gloomy historic district in which he lived.

His rickety old house, bleak and in constant need of maintenance, stood as a testimony to gloom and melancholy in a way few structures can, and gave every appearance of spirits residing within. Most of the shutters, dingy and worn, barely clung to the clapboard siding. The frayed curtains, hanging crooked in the windows, announced to all who gazed upon the façade that the home suffered from loneliness and neglect, which mirrored its occupant. Upon entering the house, guests, which were rare, experienced an instant bombardment of scents and aromas, not all of them pleasant, which appeared to attack the nasal passages and taste buds from all directions. Cloves of garlic hung at each outer doorframe to ward off vampires. Each room sported a different herb, placed in a variety of dirty containers adorned with cobwebs, indicating they had not moved from their location for an undetermined amount of time. Scents of dill, lavender, oregano, and parsley mixed with the smell of mold, curtains in need of washing, and the old wooden floor covered with dust which swirled up in little whirlwinds as one walked from room to room to dismal, depressing room.

"The herbs keep the evil spirits at bay, monsieur," he often mumbled. If no guest was present, he mumbled it to himself.

He *always* threw salt over his shoulder, no matter whether he spilled any or not, and always in the same manner: Granules pinched between the thumb and first two fat, stubby fingers of his right hand, then tossed over his left shoulder as he muttered "Le Grace." He never walked under a ladder, lived in wretched fear every Friday the 13th, and avoided black cats at all costs. Above all, he religiously made sure his closet door was securely closed at night before retiring for bed.

Never remarrying after the death of his pungent wife, he found companionship in a large gray cat, which he named Neptune. Oddly enough, the cat never vocalized in the form which we humans refer to as a "meow." Neptune made no such noise, ever. He purred, of that there is no doubt. But oddly, this gray cat, large and magnificent in appearance, was for all practical purposes mute.

Jules and Neptune spent nearly every hour of the day together. At dawn each morning, Jules awakened to the familiar sensation of Neptune rubbing against his stubbly whiskers. Jules typically spent a moment or two rubbing the cat's ears, then both arose from the bed for a mutual breakfast. They took walks together each morning, ate lunch together, and spent the afternoon together as Jules read from his voluminous library while Neptune sat at his feet napping. Then each night, Neptune jumped upon the bed, found a comfortable place, circled around it a few times, and laid down. Meanwhile, Jules checked the closet door, making sure it was fully closed and latched. Afterward, he crawled into bed next to his friend, turned off the light upon his nightstand, rolled over toward Neptune, and drifted off to sleep.

This routine played out every day and night with little variation. The two friends were inseparable and lived together in constant peace and harmony.

Yet one night, one fateful, awful night, everything went awry…

Late that steamy summer evening, Jules was consumed with digging around in his closet for something. No one knows for certain what object he wished to find, but he apparently spent considerable time in the tiny vestiary looking and moving and moving and looking. When his search proved fruitless, he slammed the door to his closet and disgustedly crawled into bed for the evening.

Looking around, he noticed Neptune was missing from his usual nocturnal location.

"Neptune? Neptune?"

No sign of the cat.

Feeling the covers, noting them to be cool, it appeared Neptune hadn't been in his spot since morning.

"Come on, you silly *chat*, it's time to retire. No more of your hide-and-seek *blague*, my friend."

When the cat still did not jump onto the bed, Jules rose and looked all around the house, calling Neptune's name.

"Come on, Neptune, I am not amused, monsieur."

After several minutes, Jules returned to his bed chamber, more irritated than before. Scratching his head and looking around the room, Jules mumbled a few words cursing the cat for not appearing. He crawled into bed, pulled a sheet over him, then turned out the light with a heavy sigh.

Had he thought of checking his closet, he would have found the cat, sitting at the door, waiting faithfully for Jules to open it. Poor Neptune, trusting Jules to take care of him, waited what must have felt like hours for his human to open the door so he could take his place on the bed. When Jules did not come to free Neptune after such a long time, the cat must have begun to panic and decided to seek freedom. He bumped the door with his head. It did not budge. So, the cat bumped the door again. As it was not completely latched from Jules' disgusted slam, after the second nudge from Neptune, the creaky old door swung slowly open.

A light sleeper, Jules was awakened by a dull thud, the first bump of Neptune's head against the closet door. Jules instantly sat up in bed.

"Wh... who's th-th-there?"

Certain it was some murderous creature breaking free, he pulled the sheet up close to his chin and lay there, eyes glued to the closet, shivering with fright.

"D-D-Don't come out here! I'll... I'll hit you with..."

Trembling, Jules looked around, seeing nothing defensive nearby.

"I'll hit you with something!"

With the second bump, the door slowly swung open with an eerie creaking noise, and the terrified Jules drew in a deep breath to scream.

Neptune, in a severe panic from being stuck in the closet, leapt up onto the bed with his claws out to make certain he didn't slip. He landed directly on Jules' leg, his claws digging through the light sheet and into Jules' skin.

Thinking he had been grabbed by whatever monster lurked in his now-open closet, Jules let out his terrified scream.

"Noooooooooooo!"

The next day, the neighbors noticed Jules was absent from his daily walk with Neptune. Concerned about his well-being, one kind Samaritan contacted the constable. Upon breaking into the home, the neighbor and constable found poor Jules, dead in his bed from failure of the heart. Next to him sat Neptune, rubbing against his friend, waiting for him to awaken.

Poor Jules. Poor Neptune.

While that tale frightens me to the core, it pales in comparison to the fate of Madeline Jambe. She too lived alone on Toulouse Street in the French Quarter of the same city, and no one was there to render assistance when her lack of attention to The Rules resulted in her demise.

At the age of six, Madeline learned about The Rules from her sister, Phianna, three years her senior.

"Madeline, you must learn."

"Learn what, Phianna?"

"You must learn there are Rules. These Rules are for your safety... at night when the lights are off."

"Why at night?"

"Because that's when it matters. That's when this city, this neighborhood, becomes something different. I know this to be true."

Madeline let out an agitated sigh.

"Ok, Phianna, tell me these rules."

"Don't be fussy," Phianna snapped. "This is for your own good. You're old enough to know. Now pay attention..."

As Phianna recited the first rule, of closing and latching the closet door, Madeline looked around the room.

"We don't have a closet," she sighed, rolling her eyes.

"I know," Phianna groaned. "But someday you might, and if you do, always make sure it is closed and latched. Otherwise, the monsters living in your closet will come out and get you. Just remember that."

"Ok." Madeline shrugged. "What's the second rule?"

"Rule Number Two is important." Phianna moved closer to Madeline's face and quieted to a whisper as she shared the second rule.

Madeline's eyes widened and she backed away from her sister.

"Phianna, are you trying to scare me?"

"No, young sister. I'm trying to save you."

They shared the same bed, Madeline and Phianna, in a small, low-ceiling loft in the attic of their meager family home. In the heat of summer, the temperature and humidity in the attic space escalated to unbearable, stifling proportions, like trying to sleep in a boiler room on wet sheets. The tiny window in the dormer provided little relief, as New Orleans' summer conditions outside were no more bearable than the heat and humidity within the room. Young Madeline often pulled one leg out of the covers, in hopes the exposed limb might offer some cooling relief.

"Mind the leg, Madeline," Phianna always whispered. "Remember, he's always under the bed, ready to grab it."

Phianna somehow always knew when her younger sister uncovered her leg. Slowly, begrudgingly, Madeline slipped her leg back under the covers.

One summer morning, when Madeline was nine, she woke up to find herself alone in bed. Normally, the sisters awakened at nearly the same time. If one awoke first, she would then reach over and touch the other, so they started their day together.

Obviously not so on this day.

Looking around the room, there was no sign of her sister. Thinking Phianna simply arose early and went downstairs, Madeline rolled over to drift back to sleep... until she heard her mother calling.

"Madeline! Phianna! Come down and eat your breakfast!"

Madeline's eyes popped open.

Did Phianna slip downstairs without Mother seeing her?

Madeline sat up and looked around the attic space again. Phianna's clothes and shoes from the previous day still lay in a heap on the chair across the room.

She would never have gone downstairs without being properly dressed. Where could she be?

Madeline jumped out of bed, looked toward the dresser, looked to the window, then stopped.

Under the bed... She might be hiding from me...

Madeline turned and walked slowly to Phianna's side of the bed. She looked down at her feet, to make sure nothing was reaching out from underneath to grab her.

It's daylight now. Nothing should grab me...

Carefully examining Phianna's disheveled side of the bed, she noticed a little tear in the fitted sheet. Like the kind of tear a fingernail would make if it gripped the sheet hard. Then she saw another one. And another. Together, they were arranged as if several fingers gripped the sheets hard... really hard.

Under the bed... I gotta look under the bed...

Slowly, Madeline got down on her knees by the bed.

Mustering up her courage, she leaned down and grabbed the hem of the old, tattered quilt under which the girls slept.

Breathing hard, she lay down flat, with the side of her head on the floor, so she could see underneath once she lifted the quilt.

Taking a deep breath, she mustered up her courage.

"On three... One..."

Her eyes were wide open.

"Two..."

She grasped the hem.

"*Three!*"

Madeline yanked the old quilt up and looked under the bed.

There, in the middle of the floor, which she noticed was surprisingly void of dust, lay a dingy white sock. But it didn't look right. Madeline reached in and grabbed the sock to pull it toward her. Something was in it. She pulled it close to her face.

The sock had a foot still in it. Phianna's foot.

It took only a moment for her to scream.

Years later, the year 1932 as a matter of fact, the summer once again brought unbearable heat and humidity, seemingly worse than the familiar boiler-room-on-wet-sheets feeling. Despite the extreme heat, Madeline slept every night fully covered by a sheet and light quilt, the same old tattered quilt she shared with her sister so many years before.

No longer did she suffer through the nights in an attic space. She lived in a proper house on Toulouse Street, boasting two bedrooms, a kitchen, parlor, and study. Each room, gaily wallpapered and filled with light from drapeless windows, smelled of lavender and fresh flowers. Yet each evening, as the shadows grew long, the house took on an air of foreboding, which rattled Madeline to her core.

During the sultry New Orleans summer nights, while the temperature in her bedroom climbed to an uncomfortable level, she never uncovered any part of her body to release some heat. All it took was remembering her poor departed sister's words...

Mind the leg, Madeline.

One day, in hopes of bringing about blessed relief from the stifling heat and sleepless nights, Madeline went to the appliance store a few blocks from her home. The tiny bell above the door rang joyously as she entered.

"Ah, Miss Jambe!" The store owner clapped his hands as he walked quickly toward her, "How may I help Madame today?"

"Hello, Mr. Le Bon." Madeline nodded. "I am shopping for a large fan, as I find myself in need of relief of this stifling heat wave."

"Aha, my lady, come this way, please. I have some fans near the counter."

Le Bon led Madeline to a display case where several large metal fans stood ready. Madeline folded her arms as she silently studied each unit. Three were small, with actuating arms to rotate the aim of the spinning blades, left then right then left again, to oscillate the airflow throughout the room. Another was a large metal box with a six-blade fan of imposing proportions inside. The fifth, largest of all, was a round fan resting upon a heavy conical base, with each of its four blades nearly eighteen inches in length.

"How about this large round one, Mr. Le Bon? I like the looks of it."

Le Bon's eyes widened.

"Ah, Miss Jambe, this is the new 1932 Griffe model by Le Zephyr Fan Company," he proclaimed, gesturing. "There's much iron and strength in this unit. It is by far their best fan and moves a tremendous amount of air. Would you like to see it run?"

"Yes please!" Madeline nodded.

Le Bon leaned over and moved the lever switch at the base.

"This is a three-speed fan, Madame. This is the low setting." Le Bon smiled as the fan spun up to its lowest speed.

After a moment, Madeline scowled.

"I'm sure this speed would be fine for stirring the air during spring or autumn, Mr. Le Bon. But I believe I wish to see the higher speeds, as the heat of this summer requires something more robust."

"Of course, Madame. I will switch to the medium speed to see if you like it better."

Le Bon moved the switch then stood back smiling with his hands folded over his stomach as he watched Madeline's reaction to the fan.

After a moment, again Madeline scowled.

"Please show me its highest speed."

Hesitating and looking around, Le Bon nodded, then moved the switch to high speed. The fan instantly spun up to a roar as papers on the nearby sales counter flew in all directions.

"I believe I like it at that speed!" Madeline yelled above the roar of the fan.

She leaned forward to point at something on the fan. Le Bon yelled, "Madame!" and grabbed her hand as he leaned over and turned off the roaring appliance. Still holding on, he patted her hand with his.

"Excusez moi, Miss Jambe." Le Bon stumbled with his words as sweat broke out on his head, "The frame around the blades of this unit... the openings, they are quite large... so large, a hand as small and delicate as yours could have easily slipped through... the blades could have cut you most terribly..."

"It's quite alright," Madeline reassured, withdrawing her hand as Le Bon regained his composure. "I would like to buy this."

"Very well, Madame." Le Bon smiled as he ran his fingers through his hair, then led her to the sales counter. "It is very heavy, and I would recommend you permit me to deliver it to your home later today."

Madeline agreed.

When Mr. Le Bon arrived with the fan, Madeline had him lug the large unit down the hall to her bedroom.

"I'd like to have the fan blow directly on me while I sleep," she instructed him.

Le Bon stopped and looked at her.

"Miss Jambe, may I please suggest you reconsider the orientation of the fan? You saw at the shop how forcefully it blew, scattering the papers resting upon the sales counter. I believe you would find it most uncomfortable to be exposed to such high velocity air as you attempt to sleep."

"What do you suggest?" Madeline inquired.

"I believe you would like the performance of the fan if it faced the other way."

"The other way? How then would I get any benefit from the fan and the great volume of air it displaces?"

"Madame, a fan of this nature draws a tremendous

amount of air from behind it in order to create the great wind emanating from the front. If you were to place the unit near the foot of your bed, with its discharge set to blow into the hall, it will draw the air from your open windows through your bedroom in a most comfortable manner, then push it down the hall. The motor on this model is very powerful and will easily pull the air through the room to cool sufficiently without you having to endure the winds at the outlet."

"I understand," Madeline agreed. "Please place it as you recommend."

Le Bon placed the great fan about eighteen inches from the foot of Madeline's bed. Satisfied, she gave him an extra gratuity for his assistance then saw him out.

That night, she prepared for bed with great excitement. Hoping to finally sleep throughout the night with relief from the heat, she turned on the huge fan, immediately switching it to the highest speed position. Turning slowly at first, the fan blades began to displace great amounts of air until the motor reached top speed. Blowing toward the door and down the hall, the gale of wind nearly slammed her bedroom door shut with great force. Luckily Madeline saw the door begin to close and managed to grab a paperweight from her dresser to act as a doorstop. Satisfied, she crawled into bed, feeling the night air sweep across her as she pulled her covers up over her body.

Mind the leg, Madeline.

The roar of the great fan drowned out all other sounds, and Madeline managed to fall asleep.

At some point in the night, lying on her right side, Madeline awoke to something tugging at her sheet and quilt. It seemed gentle at first, just a couple of light tugs, then felt more forceful. As she gained her senses from her deep sleep, she realized her left leg had somehow escaped from the protective cover of the sheet and quilt.

Mind the leg, Madeline.

At once, the old, tattered quilt was forcefully pulled from the bed, and to Madeline's horror, she realized something had hold of her exposed leg, pulling her to the floor.

She screamed, "Phianna, help me!" as if her sister still slept with her in the same bed.

Madeline clawed at her bedding, digging her fingernails into the fitted sheet.

"No no no! Please leave me alone!"

Screaming and crying, she clawed furiously, pulling the fitted sheet loose. Unable to maintain her grip, she fell face down upon the floor, dragged farther by the as yet unseen beast.

"Why have you returned for me? Was my sister not enough?" she cried as she thrashed about, looking for some way to break free.

She let out a great scream as she felt the jaws of the beast clamp down into her feet, severing her toes in one large bite. She gasped, screamed again, then passed out as her blood began to pool around her body.

Within several minutes, a night watchman broke down her front door to gain entrance. Despite the sound of the great fan, the neighbors next door, who also slept with their windows open, heard her frightful screams, and summoned the authorities. Running back to Madeline's bedroom, the officers were greeted by a gruesome sight. The great fan, positioned so close to her bed, had pulled the old, tattered quilt through the blades, shooting the ragged remains into the hall. The sheet, wrapped around her leg, pulled into the fan as well, taking her leg with it. Her femur stopped the blades of the great fan from turning, which was now humming as the motor overheated. Alas, they were too late to save her, as the blood loss had been too rapid, too great.

As the night watchman turned off the fan to prevent a fire, the other officer looked at the ripped fitted sheet on her bed, then bent down over the deceased woman to assess the situation.

"Poor lady. It must have been awful to be pulled into the fan like that," the officer sighed.

"Yeah, this is terrible," the night watchman moaned. "Judging by the rips in the sheet, she put up quite a fight."

"Too bad."

The two men crouched in silence over the body of the woman.

"Her fingernails don't make sense though," the night watchman said, looking closely at the bloody scene.

"What do you mean?"

The night watchman leaned over and lifted up Madeline's left hand.

"I just mean her fingernails are not very long. Certainly not long enough to put those deep scratch marks on what's left of her leg…"

THE PEELER

—— • ● • ——

No, I won't do it.

No, please, I beg you.

No, I – I can't bear the agony of re-telling the story. Here in this bed, I remain in a weakened condition. The stitches holding my flesh together are but a few days old, and the pain in my lungs and back - it grips me, holds me, squeezes the breath out of me. It's all too much. It's all... all too much.

I'm – I'm horrified by the details, horrified to relive it for the sake of sharing the story yet again. Horrified to have been there. Simply – simply horrified.

Honestly at this point, I'm afraid to go to sleep. I'm afraid that when I close my eyes, I will see the events unfold again, for the entire scene has played out before my closed eyes each night, each night since that dreadful, awful evening.

No.

No.

I said "*no.*"

Quit looking at me like that.

Sigh.

Alas... I know that what I have to say, the story I have to tell, is important. Therefore, I must, with every bit of strength I possess, share the details of what happened. Maybe if I tell it one more time, the nightmares will end, and I may be permitted that great luxury, that sweet benefit, of restful slumber.

I believe the first time I became aware of the series of

brutal murders, it was due to the local newspaper and television stations covering the story. Unfortunately, the daily news was always full of reports of killings, attacks, and other forms of human brutality. However, such events always happened in places far away, towns in some other state or county. Never had such evil come to this town, or at least not that anyone alive could remember. I recalled in my teens hearing that somewhere in my ancestry, there had been a murder, but the details were never explained to me clearly. It was just one of those skeletons in the closet presumably from Wild West days, kinda like when you're related to someone like Doc Holliday or the Clantons. Therefore, I typically ignored modern stories of heinous events in faraway places with the same distant acknowledgment as those old cowboy tales.

Yet, the evil arrived. Here, in my town, Death lurked, and Fear hung oppressive and cold over everyone, like the low, frightening clouds and ominous Bachian rumble of an approaching storm.

The *Local Daily Visiter*, that hopeless rag of a newspaper with one word of its name intentionally misspelled, claimed to be the first to call the killer "The Peeler." No doubt the moniker stuck after they revealed the recurring morbid condition of each victim. Each poor deceased soul was found with the skin on their fingers removed and a large abdominal wound, caused by some heinous blade wielded by the brutal attacker. Within the wound was always found a peeler, that sharp utensil most commonly used to remove the skin from potatoes. No doubt it had been used to skin the fingers of the victims. I understood why the press called him The Peeler, but still I couldn't help but think someone could have come up with a better name.

Countless psychiatrists, psychologists, lawyers, doctors, and even clergy weighed in on the meaning and significance of the peeler; the tool of a cook or chef, used so heinously and shoved in the gaping, atrocious wound of each victim. Each so-called expert tried to explain how the killer was most likely abused or somehow mentally snapped during military service, and that he needed psychiatric help immediately upon apprehension. And with each article, each quotation from a doctor, each press conference by some preacher who eventually got around to asking for money, I just shook my head and thought, "They just need to kill the crazy son of a bitch."

With that bit of background properly shared, I believe I can bring you up to the most recent events, the situation in which I found myself those few nights ago, and the madness which developed most rapidly.

I left my place of employment late that evening, the sun having already set by the time I arrived at the home of my parents, on the city's west side. Due to a recent change in jobs, my financial situation became somewhat tenuous, so my parents permitted me to stay with them these past three months. I occupied the same bedroom where I lived as a child, and I'm fairly certain the uncomfortable twin mattress upon which my body rested each night was the same as well. I had also broken up with my girlfriend of two years. Well, I guess that's not completely accurate. She left. Just left. No note, no phone call. One day, she and all her stuff were just gone.

The living conditions at Mom and Dad's place were uncomfortable at best. I felt like a failure, having lost a job and ended a relationship within a very short amount of time. My parents were not unkind, but I felt a tension there, as an invader in their private lives which they had carved out upon my departure from the home so many years prior. Dad was still as quiet as he had ever been. Mom was still a very tense person, always mad at someone about something they said or a certain way someone looked at her. I had heard all her complaints about neighbors and people at church for years, so her rants were nothing new. Yet all remained pleasant enough, I guess, and I was thankful to be allowed to stay there until my financial situation improved.

Back to that night…

As I pulled into the driveway, I saw my parents standing on the front porch with great concern on their faces. I parked and got out quickly to discover the source of their consternation. Dad, seated in his favorite porch-sitting chair, held his double-barrel shotgun between his knees, proceeding to wipe it down as he eyed my approach. Next to him, on the short round table normally reserved for glasses of sweetened iced tea, sat two boxes of ammunition. One contained the shells for his shotgun. The other had bullets for my pistol, which also lay on the table next to an empty chair. Mom crouched behind Dad, plugging in the police scanner.

"Sit down, Son." Dad nodded to the empty chair.

"What the hell is going on, Dad?" I asked.

"Look over yonder."

Dad cocked his head toward the hillside a couple of blocks away to the east.

In the gathering dark, over the rooftops of our neighbors' houses, I could see the red and blue flashing beacons atop police cars; lots of police cars.

"They think they may know where that murdering bastard is," Dad growled. "That's awfully close. I want to be prepared just in case they didn't actually get him and he's still on the loose."

I immediately sat down in the chair and loaded my pistol. Mom turned on the scanner then placed it between us, on the table amongst the boxes of shells and bullets.

"Ellen, you get inside and find yourself a good place to hide. If this goes bad, I don't want him coming after you. And turn off that porch light."

Mom turned and went inside without saying a word. Then in an instant, all was blackness as she turned off the light.

"Hopefully that scanner will lock in on any police transmissions so we can hear what's going on," Dad muttered.

Our eyes strained in the darkness, trained on the array of red and blue lights on the hillside. As we concentrated to listen for anything the police said on the scanner, a trickle of sweat ran down the side of my face. I finished loading my pistol as we listened to three or four voices trying to talk at once on the scanner.

One voice ordered everyone to hold tight until further backup arrived. Another voice thought eight officers was enough, and one voice told both sons of bitches to shut up and move. Then suddenly they must have entered the house. We heard one *"holy shit,"* one *"dammit,"* and one *"aw hell."* Then a brief silence.

"We've got a body with a goddamn peeler shoved in it. This guy's been dead for a while."

"Any sign of the killer anywhere?"

"No, he's gone."

Dad and I cocked our weapons.

The night around us was a suffocating pitch black at that point. The homes of the neighbors across the street were simply dark boxes that partially blocked the sight of the police cars. The closest streetlight, on a pole at the corner of our yard, had been awaiting replacement for several months. Our end of the street was black. Not just dark but black, like you're in a cave by yourself and your one and only light goes out. That kind of black.

The scanner went quiet. Dad and I looked around, but saw nothing, heard nothing.

I mean literally, we heard nothing.

In the midst of that summer heat wave, the bugs should have been sounding off. The cicadas were supposed to be out, and it should have been deafening, amidst their squalling. They weren't squalling though. No dogs barked. It was as if everything around us felt the tension in the area and went into hiding.

Dad reached over and switched off the now-silent scanner.

Another drop of sweat trickled slowly down the side of my face, changing its course slightly with the contours of my skin. My shirt stuck to my body in the heat and humidity, feeling like my flesh and the fabric were intermingled. I longed for a tall glass of cold water.

Quietly, I cleared my throat.

"Dad, what if…"

"Shh! Quiet! Not a word, Son."

Suddenly we heard a loud sound from the house across the street, the Clark place. I strained to listen. It reminded me of the sound of something large hitting the floor. Or maybe some*one* hitting the floor. Then more noise, like stomping. Like a scuffle. Then glass broke. Then more glass broke.

"Should we go over there, Dad?" I whispered.

"No, Son. You wouldn't be able to see anything. Better to stay here."

Then there was silence. Whatever ruckus happened at the Clark place, it was done.

Suddenly we heard the screen door of that house creak open then slam closed. But in the blackness of that night, we couldn't see anything. Someone either went in… or came out…

Then more deafening silence; no breeze, no birds, no cicadas. Nothing rustled, not the slightest sound from any direction.

You know how when a big storm is coming and everything goes quiet? It seems most of the time you can hear a dog bark or a loud car or a train horn or something like that. Not this time. It was like being locked in a sound-proof box. My ears were pounding, which didn't help much as I strained to listen.

We barely breathed.

Suddenly Dad flinched.

"Something's moving," he whispered as he leveled his gun, aiming into the blackness.

"Where, Dad? I don't see anything," I whispered back, straining to see.

"I don't see it. I don't hear it... I *feel* it. Something is moving somewhere... somewhere in front of us."

After several moments of straining to see or hear anything, a sound broke the silence; a most awful sound.

It was a gasp, a gurgle, a terrible, gut-wrenching sound of pain and death. And it came from Dad.

I looked, barely seeing through the darkness as his body suddenly stiffened. His arms, thrusting out in front of him, dropped his shotgun. His eyes, large and round, showed terror and agony as something, some unknown act or device or... or weapon... took the life from him.

As I began to turn, something huge, sharp, and metallic thrust into my body from behind. I shuddered all over as this thing stabbed deeper into me, puncturing my lung. In an instant, I realized that this murderer, this devil incarnate, this man of horror, had somehow managed to sneak up behind Dad and me during our vigil, to take us as his next victims. This beast must have attacked our neighbor then came for us.

I fell forward as the knife was pulled from my back by the assailant. Gasping for air, I fell forward out of the chair but caught myself and rolled over. I was still coherent enough to look around.

In the next moment, I heard our front door open, and the porch light came on, illuminating everything. There was Dad, slumped over in his chair, dead or dying. His shotgun, lying near me, hadn't even discharged.

And there before me stood my murderer, the one who so many had discussed, the one who so many sought, the one those officers two blocks away wanted so badly. The devil incarnate.

I knew my murderer.

It was Mom.

In her right hand, dripping with blood – my blood, and that of my father – she held the knife that she used to stab us. In her left hand, she held two potato peelers; one intended for Dad… and one for me.

"Mom?" I gasped. "Mom, why?"

"You were in my way. I had such a nice life after you left, teaching people lessons, and your dad he needed to be taught a lesson and now you were sitting here trying to kill me and you both needed to be taught a lesson – just like Mrs. Clark that bitch needed to be taught a lesson and Mr. Babcock your old principal over there where all the police cars are – you remember he once sent you home because of your ratty clothes – well I did my best to keep you in good clothes but obviously it wasn't good enough for him!"

"Mom? That happened over ten years ago. I was just a kid and we were poor. You've been mad at him all this time?"

"I stay mad at everyone I stayed mad at him and mad at Mrs. Clark – she always thought her flowers were prettier than mine and Dan Davis looked at my shoes once when I passed him so I killed him and I don't like people looking at my shoes and your damn girlfriend didn't leave you – I didn't like her but don't you worry they will never find her I took care of that there will be no body to find with her."

"You – you killed my Sophie?"

"I didn't just kill her," she growled as her lips curled into a horrible smile.

"But, Mom." I tried to speak. I wanted to ask. My head was spinning, and I felt sick. Blood pooled up around me as I tried to move. "Mom, why… why the… why this peeler thing?"

"My sister," she said, lowering her eyes for a moment.

In that moment, as blood pooled around me and the

world seemed to spin, making me sick, I saw the intensity fade from my mother's eyes.

"Mom..."

She snapped her head back up, and her eyes burned into me.

"My sister, my sister, Eleanor you remember hearing about a murder that occurred in our family – it was Eleanor my sister she was sick she was weak she spent her life in a wheelchair and couldn't walk – she was fooled by a guy who pretended to be interested in her and he – "

She stopped for a moment. I tried to catch my breath.

"He took her someplace and there were lots of guys there and they had their way with her and beat her and hurt her then they killed her but I knew who they were and I tracked down each one and killed them and hid their identity by skinning their fingers so they couldn't be identified by fingerprints – a peeler works really well for taking skin off of someone – and I wanted to keep killing so I did and decided to stick the peeler in them as a memento of my work."

She stopped talking, breathing hard. She looked down at her hands, the knife dripping blood, the peelers in the other hand.

She looked at me.

"But, Mom, you can stop. You don't have to kill anymore. You've avenged your sister. It's done."

She stared at me, cocking her head as if trying to understand me.

"I can stop?"

"Yes, Mom, you can stop."

I gasped for air.

She looked down at her hands again then looked back at me.

"I – I – I can st – "

I was afraid to move, afraid to say anything. Was I getting through to her?

Her eyes widened.

"No!"

Her eyes, red with hatred, glared as she took a step toward me, thrusting the bloody knife forward.

So I aimed my pistol. And fired twice. That was enough.

Now leave me alone…

SHOULD HAVE STOPPED IN QUINCY

— •●• —

Hugh Franks went too far. Driving along Highway 28, taking the "scenic route" from Spokane to Seattle, he should have stopped in Quincy for the night. A town of about 8,000, Quincy had several nice hotels where he could have stayed. Worried about his expense account, though, Hugh drove past each one. He had made up his mind that Rock Island, another twenty-two miles down the road, would be the place to stop for the night. Later, as he drove through Rock Island, however, he realized the town was about one-fifth the size of Quincy and had no hotels. His only choice was to go another ten miles to Wenatchee, where he knew plenty of inexpensive lodging was available.

There was only one problem, and it was a big one: Hugh was getting sleepy. Leaving Rock Island behind him, he stared into the darkness to his left, knowing the Columbia River roared there, beyond where he could see...

Headlights! A car horn!

Shit, I'm in the other lane!

He didn't know how long he had been asleep at the wheel, or how many feet, yards, or hell, miles he had driven completely asleep.

Come on, Franks. Just a little bit to go. Dammit, I should have stopped in Quincy.

It wasn't long before the lights of the towns which made up the greater Wenatchee area came into view. Appleyard to the west, and East Wenatchee on the other side of the river, then finally Wenatchee itself.

Hugh knew of a cheap little hotel on Mission Street called the Columbia View Suites. The whole place lived a double lie: it had no view of the Columbia River, and the rooms were far from suites. The building had no personality whatsoever. The walls were constructed of concrete blocks, and the rooms, dark and depressing with thin commercial carpet on the floor, smelled and felt musty, like the drain for the air conditioner had plugged years ago and all the condensate was being blown back into the room.

Hugh stayed in this dump plenty of times over his years of traveling for work. Bob, the gray-haired desk clerk, positioned safely behind bullet-proof glass, looked up from his girlie magazine and smiled as he recognized the sleepy soul walking toward him through the dimly lit, smoke-filled lobby.

"Hugh Franks! It's been a while!"

Yeah, and there's a good reason for that.

"Hi, Bob. Yes, it has indeed. Glad to be back."

Liar.

"It's been one of those nights, Bob. I need a room before I fall asleep standing here."

"No problem, Hugh. Second floor, 217."

"Thanks, Bob."

"Get some sleep!"

Too tired for stairs, Hugh slogged over to the elevator. Pressing the Up button, Hugh heard the hydraulics roar to life. From previous experience, Hugh knew the elevator ride from the first floor to the second took exactly ten seconds. Tonight, it was going to be the longest ten seconds he had yet to encounter.

Finally on the second floor, the elevator stopped with a jolt, the doors opened, and Hugh stepped out. An ice machine rattled and vibrated in a cubby hole next to the elevator. Directly across from both noisy contraptions was Room 217.

Great. I get to listen to these things.

Hugh put the key in the door and as he began to turn it, he heard yelling down the hallway to his right.

And I get to listen to them too.

The door clicked, and with a big yawn, Hugh walked into the wet air of his spacious accommodation. The small color television on its little rolling cart had been left on, though not tuned to a station, with the volume up. Hugh set down his suitcase on the ratty-looking recliner, shut off the TV, then sat down on the side of the little twin bed. The metal springs creaked, protesting his middle-aged weight as he sat, removing his shoes and taking off his shirt.

Gotta be at this meeting tomorrow. I can't oversleep. Gotta get this account.

Once his pants were off and tossed across the room, he slid under the sheet and thin blanket. He was asleep before his head hit the pillow.

It was a fitful sleep that night for him, not restful and full of pleasant dreams as he had hoped. His brain and body were too tired, and all pleasantness was denied in those first few hours of slumber.

Car nearly running off the road. Headlights in my eyes. Bang bang bang! Should have stopped in Quincy. Help! Help! Help 210! Did I ask for a wakeup call? Meeting tomorrow afternoon. Hope they become a new customer. Better hotels in Quincy. Bang bang bang! Help 215! Help! Help! Gotta get to the Seattle airport by 4:00pm. Don't want to have to stay an extra night. Should have stayed in Quincy. BANG BANG BANG! Help 217! Help 217! Open up!

Hugh twitched then jolted awake. He sat up in bed.

Did somebody just bang on the door? I heard something about 217.

Then he heard it, banging on another room down the hall.

"220! Help! Anybody in there? 220 open up! I need help!"

It was a woman's voice, and she sounded like she was in a panic. She kept going down the hall, banging on doors, trying to get someone to answer.

Hugh jumped out of bed and ran to the door. He squinted, looking through the peephole to see if he could see anyone. He saw a dark shape or shapes and movement down the hall, which he could only guess was the woman doing the yelling and banging on doors.

She's in trouble. Maybe someone is after her. Maybe she's been kidnapped and has gotten away from him. She's trying to get away. I've got to do something.

He reached for the dead bolt on the door then stopped.

Wait a minute. If she's trying to get away from someone, why isn't she running out of the hotel? Why would she be trying to get into another room? If she hides in a room, whoever is with her can't be far behind.

Maybe it's all a sham. Maybe they are in cahoots together. Maybe he's right there, and as soon as I open the door, he runs in and I get robbed. Or worse. Maybe they are murderers, and I could get tied up, stuffed in a trunk, and taken somewhere remote to be tortured and killed.

She should be trying to get away, not just into another room in the hotel.

Hugh closed his eyes and listened. The banging had stopped. She quit calling out room numbers for help.

Slowly, quietly, Hugh turned the handle on the dead bolt. Breathing hard, he then slowly, silently, turned the knob to open his door.

This is it. Don't know what I'm going to see here, but I gotta do this.

Slowly, quietly, he opened the door just enough to poke his head out into the hallway. The normally boisterous ice machine had shut off and the elevator was silent. Looking down the dark, dismal corridor, he saw nothing. Then he heard something. It was quiet, almost whispering. It sounded a bit like the same woman's voice.

"Let go of me. Let go of me. I said let go."

Then somewhere down the hallway, a door clicked shut, and there was no more sound.

Hugh shuddered.

Should I go down and tell Bob? Should I call the police? What would I tell them? What really happened here tonight? Was the yelling for real, or did their plan backfire? Did he grab her? Had they been staying on this floor? Or was that the door to the stairwell I heard click? A woman is either in serious trouble, or a couple of cons struck out tonight.

Hugh stumbled back over to the bed and sat down, holding his head in his hands, trying to figure out what to do.

It just makes no sense. If this was a lady really in trouble, she would have run out of the hotel rather than just trying to hole up in someone else's room. There's no just way running into someone else's room would help, because whoever was after her or had kidnapped her couldn't be far behind. He would know what was up by hearing all the banging then show up. And then whoever would be harboring her would be in danger of their lives. It just couldn't be that. I think I just dodged a bullet, and someone is using these sleepy travelers and their good nature to act out some sort of scam to get into someone's room and rob them. That's gotta be it. I'm glad I waited to open the door. I'm glad I didn't end up being a victim in all of this. Shameful.

Hugh crawled back into bed, turned off the light, and rolled over to get a few more hours of sleep.

Another round of banging on the door jolted him awake.

Hugh wasn't released to leave the hotel until about 3:00 p.m. that afternoon. With red eyes and disheveled clothes, he waded through the police cars, the spectators, and the ambulance with something in the back wrapped in bloody sheets.

He had missed his meeting. He was going to miss his flight in Seattle.

He sat in his rental car, trembling hands on the wheel, staring blankly ahead at nothing.

Should have stopped in Quincy...

JUMPER

At first it seemed like a good idea
To jump
To end it all
To be done
But within a fraction of a second
It became clear
The fall was becoming
More and more scary
And I wished I would have never jumped
And the ground
Kept coming closer
And I kept falling faster
And I knew
There was no way I was going to survive this
And I wondered
Why I felt like jumping in the first place
As the ground kept coming faster
And faster
And faster
And there was no air in my lungs for screaming
As my arms and legs flailed about
Uncontrollably
And it began to hurt
As my limbs were pulled back
Farther and farther behind me
As the ground
Continued to come flying up toward me
And I decided

To hit face first
So I could watch
As the ground
Kept coming
Faster
Faster
And I wished I was still up on that balcony
And I saw the people watching me
And screaming
As I h–

MARKED

$\bullet\!\bullet\!\bullet$

When I decided to call it quits on the proverbial rat race and move to the Ozarks hill country of southwest Missouri, I could never have guessed what awaited me.

Just a wide spot in the road, the tiny hamlet of Thermal Springs existed on the verge of being a ghost town, the lonely remains of a once-flourishing community that originally owed its existence to a local hot mineral water source. The spring reportedly dried up when a couple of greedy aldermen decided to try to get more water flow, courtesy of a few sticks of dynamite. In their misbegotten efforts to further develop the town, they blew out the bottom of the water table, and almost overnight, the community died. No spring, no visitors. The town's structures decayed and fell, and eventually the area just became known as "Thermal."

A few old structures from the little settlement's lively past still stood, but just barely. Half a dozen houses and mobile homes, each desperately in need of a fresh coat of paint, lined the dusty gravel road through what Thermal used to be, indicating some folks still scratched out a life there. Most of the dwellings, with old cars and mounds of junk in their yards, stood as lonely reminders that a thriving community once inhabited the overgrown fields lining the main road. The structure originally housing the post office still stood, though with its rotting boards and leaning disposition, it was clearly just one windstorm away from being flattened. Trees grew in the middle of the foundation where the hotel once welcomed dozens of visitors every day. Each sunrise looked promising as another chance for the remains of the town, but each sunset cast lonesome, dismal shadows, as doors locked and drapes were drawn.

The only real sign of life in Thermal was the Gibbons Grocery, a small, vintage 1940s general store with two old gas pumps outside. If a gallon of milk and a loaf of bread was all one needed, Gibbons was sufficient. Otherwise, a thirty-minute drive to nearby Cassville was required for a full-blown grocery run or dinner at a café.

None of the locals knew what to think when I moved into Thermal's old, abandoned schoolhouse on sixty acres and began renovating the wooden building into living quarters. While still in Michigan, I was intrigued when I noticed it in the country real estate magazine. Upon making my first trip to the area to see the old schoolhouse, as well as Thermal itself, I couldn't help but feel it was the singular bright spot in the county. The schoolhouse stood tall and proud about three-hundred feet from the main road, situated on the western edge of an open twenty acres of land, with another forty wooded acres adjacent. The distinct sunken driveway, formed from the hundreds of horse-drawn carts which traveled its path over countless decades, reminded me of what must have been scores of children who lived too far away to walk. Surrounded by massive old oak and hickory trees spaced about twenty-five feet apart, the old schoolhouse had entry doors on the front and back, with two large double-hung windows on each of the four walls.

Inside, any section of wall without a window contained a chalkboard, some in better condition than others. Near the middle of the single large room stood the original cast-iron wood-fired stove used to heat the place. Standing nearly as tall as me, it seemed grossly oversized for the task of providing warmth. Nonetheless, I was happy to discover it to be in good order, as I intended to let it do its job when cold weather prevailed.

I bought the place that very day.

I don't wish to give the impression of being overly blessed with money to buy and fix up the old building. On the contrary, I had just enough to get by for a while. Upon the death of my mother, my last living relative, my inheritance amounted to not much more than a few thousand dollars and a full set of genuine silver flatware, of which my mother had been very proud. A wedding gift from her grandmother, who first acquired it when she got married back in the late 1800s, I found the set to be in excellent condition, still in its original cherry wood box. The sale of my home in Michigan funded the purchase of this wonderful place in Thermal.

I took possession of the old schoolhouse in late August, during a hot dry spell, several weeks before the coming of autumn rains. I didn't have a lot of furniture when I bought the place, so it was a fairly easy task to move in and begin to set things up. I put my bed in the northeast corner of the room, with my head against the east wall, near the window. My dresser was placed on the other side of the window, and anything needing to be hung up, which amounted to three shirts and a suit for which I had no use, hung just fine on four nails in the wall. The old original sideboard, still in excellent condition, served as a decent pantry, and I figured my mother wouldn't mind if I stored her silver flatware set on the bottom shelf.

Once aptly settled, I commenced work on the schoolhouse, making sure it was ready for winter months. As would be the case in any small town, the news spread quickly through Thermal that the man who bought the old schoolhouse was making improvements. Soon three old guys from the village began coming, albeit uninvited, to watch me work.

Every weekday morning, if the weather cooperated, these colorful fellows arrived at the same time, about 8:30. I could hear them talking as they turned into my driveway.

Each old codger carried his own folding chair, which they set up on whatever side of the building I happened to be working. They'd argue for several minutes about who would sit where then settle in to watch me.

The first guy was Ed. Nearly bald and not a tooth in his head, Ed was a veteran of the Second World War. He liked wearing an old dirty hat with "Airborne" stitched into it. I knew enough about paratroopers to realize if he indeed served in the airborne, Ed was a badass in his day. Now, he was a shriveled up little old man who liked to talk. I pretty much instantly liked Ed.

The second old geezer was Herman. Taller than Ed but just as thin, he liked letting you know he too served in the Second World War, as well as Korea. His ratty old green ball cap didn't have anything stitched in it about the Army. Instead, it proudly displayed the emblem for his favorite brand of lawn mower.

Rounding out the trio of gawkers was Earl. Never serving in the military, Earl was a stooped-over retired accountant with a mind like a steel trap. He was quiet most of the time, but when he spoke, the other two stopped talking to listen.

One day, they found out I was from Michigan, so suddenly I was called "Yank." Apparently to them, that moniker automatically meant I didn't know my ass from a hole in the ground. Then they *really* wanted to stop by and watch me work so they could critique my progress.

One evening, when my work dragged on late, well after dusk, the four of us heard animals sounding off in the hills to the south, across the hollow where Rockhouse Creek meanders through the boulder-strewn lowlands. It started with a singular low howl, guttural and several seconds in length. Then one yip. Then another. Then several more, each high-pitched. It ended up sounding like a frenzied collection of yips, barks, and cries.

"Sounds like a bunch of coyotes across the holler," I

said, without looking up.

"Those aren't coyotes, Yank. They're wolves," Earl commented.

I raised my head and made eye contact with him.

"I didn't think wolves had a high-pitched yip like that."

"They're wolves alright," Herman said, looking toward the holler. "I've heard them a bunch of times. Don't be fooled now."

"Better listen closely, in case they start sounding their approach," Earl spoke up.

Ed and Herman turned and looked at Earl then back at me.

"Approach?" I questioned. "I've never heard of coyotes – I mean wolves – getting very close to people."

"It's different here," Earl said. "Not that many of us in this area. They're a little braver. And if you're old like us boys here, you're easy pickins' for a bunch of 'em."

"Yep, speaking of which, we better git going," Herman said as he slowly rose from his seat and stretched. "I got a little ways to walk. And I'm not any faster than you two old codgers."

The other two spectators stood up and stretched for a moment as the yips and howls continued then gathered up their folding chairs and started walking away.

"Wait a minute," I called after them. "You know, I like to take walks after dark. I did it all the time back up in Michigan. Are you guys saying I could be in danger if I did so here?"

The three men looked at each other briefly then back at me.

"Do ya have a lantern?" Ed asked.

"Yes, I've got several. My favorite is an old kerosene lantern. It was my father's."

"That'll work," Herman answered. "Do you have a good stick? Like a good hickory stick to carry with you when you walk?"

I chuckled.

"This property is full of hickory trees. I'm sure I could scrounge one up."

Herman's face never changed, and apparently never saw any humor in my response.

"You're going to need it, Yank. Especially if they get a little hungry, and there's several of them. You might want to sharpen it a bit too, in case you have to poke one to get it away from you."

I agreed with a grin, as Earl walked up to me.

"Don't think this is anything funny, Yank. We're serious."

Ed and Herman stopped talking and turned to listen to Earl.

"If you think you need to take a walk around dark, you heed what we say. Ole Mrs. Briller down the holler" – Earl pointed off to the northeast as he spoke – "she lost one of her boys to wolves one night. He was in pieces when they found him the next day. And he was about your size. So, pay attention."

"Alright, I appreciate the advice." I nodded, trying to be more serious as he turned to join the other two.

"Goodnight, Yank," they called out as they slowly made their way along the sunken driveway to the main road.

As the last old man disappeared from sight, the wolves continued making noise.

They do sound closer.

I walked inside, locking the door behind me.

That night, as I lay in bed with the windows open, I listened closely for any sounds near the old schoolhouse. Hearing none, I eventually drifted off the sleep.

The next day, a Saturday, found me ten feet off the ground, confined to a ladder as I worked to repair the old wood soffit on the north side of the schoolhouse. Being a

Saturday with a slight threat of rain, my three critics had elected to stay home. Toward sunset, as the colors around me began to deepen, I considered calling it a day.

"Sure does look nice up there!"

I jumped as the sound of a female voice startled me. I turned quickly to see a short, thin old lady, hands on her hips, staring up at me. She was a sight to behold. Her hair, gray and wiry, seemed to sprout in every direction from her head. Her weather-beaten face bore a multitude of wrinkles which testified to a life of hardship. Her dress was a simple piece of homespun work, and she wore old hard-soled shoes on her feet, the kind I imagined the teacher wore in the heyday of the schoolhouse.

"Thank you, ma'am," I called out as I descended the ladder. "It's coming along."

"I didn't mean to interrupt you," she said as she inched a little closer. "But I hadn't the chance to come by and introduce myself till now. I'm Mrs. Higgins."

I wiped my hands quickly with the rag from my pocket then reached out to be neighborly.

"Very pleased to make your acquaintance, Mrs. Higgins. I'm Billy. Billy Horner."

"So pleased to meet you, Billy."

The handshake was brief, and she quickly tucked her hand back into the pocket of her dress. For the first time, I noticed her necklace. On a rough leather string were odd little shapes, smooth and off-white in color, with a hole drilled in the middle for the string. They were like shells, but not quite. I caught myself staring and changed my gaze to her smiling face.

"I live just down the road, to the east toward the holler," she continued, "and I heard about all the wonderful things you are doing for this old schoolhouse. I went to school here, you know."

"You don't say!"

"Oh yes, all twelve grades right here in this building!

We would play and sing and dance and practice our addition tables. Me and my pal Joyce chased Tommy Briller..."

"Oh yes, I've heard the name Briller," I interrupted. "Any relation to the boy I heard died one night?"

"Yes..."

Mrs. Higgins' smile suddenly left her face.

"Tommy Briller was his daddy. Joyce married him. Tommy ran off after the baby was born. Seth Briller was their boy you speak of. Of course it's not polite to speak ill of the dead, but..."

Mrs. Higgins looked down.

"But what?" I couldn't help but want to hear more.

"Seth Briller was trouble. Nothin' but trouble. That boy crossed my path a bunch of times... too many... but yes, one night –"

Across the hollow, the wolves again started their evening serenade.

Mrs. Higgins turned slightly, listening. I detected a slight grin on her face.

"They sound hungry tonight," she said quietly.

"What?"

I wasn't sure I heard her right.

She turned back to me and smiled sweetly as the sound of the wolves got louder.

"Well, I guess I'd best be on my way. Don't want to get caught out after dark, you know! It's awfully nice to meet you, Mr. Horner, and I look forward to seeing you again sometime."

"Nice to meet you too, Mrs. Higgins. Stop by any time."

"Oh, I will!" she called out over her shoulder as she raised her right arm and flicked her wrist.

I leaned over to pick up the rag for my hands and noticed the sound of the wolves had stopped. As a matter of fact, they didn't sound off again the rest of the evening.

The next day, I noticed my stock of groceries had dwindled to the point that a trip to Cassville was necessary. So, without taking notice of my near-empty gas tank, I headed to town for provisions. It wasn't until I was a few miles from Thermal I noticed the "low fuel" light on my dash was illuminated, and I wondered how long it had been glowing, and how long the needle on my gas gauge showed nearly empty.

"Damn, Horner, you gotta pay more attention to stuff down here," I fussed at myself.

I must have been on fumes as I turned into the parking lot for Gibbons Grocery. Fortunately, no one was gassing up at the 1970s-era pumps, so I pulled in and filled up the tank.

Opening the door to the old building so I could pay for my gas, I nearly knocked over Mrs. Higgins. We both let out a yell and she jumped, causing the half-gallon bottle of milk to fall out of her arms, shattering on the floor and spraying milk everywhere, including on both of us.

"Oh, Mrs. Higgins! I'm so sorry! Are you alright?" I could feel my face turning red from embarrassment.

"Oh dear!" She fussed as she stepped away from the broken glass. "Mr. Horner! My goodness you frightened me! Now look at this mess all over the floor!"

"It's okay, Mrs. Higgins." The teenager on duty smiled as he ran over with a couple of towels. "Don't worry about this mess. I'll get it cleaned up. You just go pick out another bottle of milk and don't think another thing of it."

"I'll have to wash this dress again or it'll smell like spoiled milk!" She turned and shook her finger at me. "You, young man, need to slow down! Around here, we don't move as fast as you people from – from – well, wherever you came from!"

"I came from Michigan, ma'am. And I'm dreadfully sorry about all of this."

She shook her finger at me again and stomped out the

door.

I leaned down to help the grocer pick up the broken glass.

"I guess I really made her mad," I chuckled.

"Yeah," the teenager said as he looked up at me. "I wouldn't want that ole bat mad at me. I've heard she can get pretty mean."

Together, we got the mess cleaned up. I made sure to pay for Mrs. Higgins' second bottle of milk when I settled up for my gas. Happy to have enough groceries for a while and my car's full tank, I headed home to put in a little more time on the renovation of the schoolhouse. That evening, the wolves were quiet, though while I was outside, I couldn't shake the feeling I was being watched from somewhere across the hollow.

After all the excitement of the day, I believe I fell asleep before my head hit the pillow. At one point in the middle of the night, my eyes popped open as I heard the distinct sound of scratching, short but persistent scratching, on the other side of the wall. Half awake, I lay there and listened as I felt a cool breeze blow across me, thanks to the open windows.

Must be a branch from the old tree still too long, rubbing against the house in the breeze. I'd better trim it tomorrow. Don't want it to rub through the paint.

I drifted back to sleep.

The next morning, I got up early, had my normal breakfast of scrambled eggs, toast, and coffee, then stepped outside to start working.

"Gotta be sure to cut off that branch rubbing against the house," I muttered to myself, head down as I walked.

Turning the corner, I stopped dead in my tracks. The oak tree, easily over a hundred years old with a trunk as big as a tractor tire, stood majestically about twenty-five feet from the house. The tree had been meticulously trimmed over the decades, and the lowest branches cascaded about ten feet over the rooftop. It was impossible for a branch to have been making the scratching sound I heard.

I walked quickly over to the area where the noise seemed to come from the night before. I ran my fingers along the rough wall, noticing the chipping paint easily detectable against my fingertips. About midway down, I found two long scratches, going down from right to left at an angle. I ran my fingers along the contours. They weren't deep, just enough to scratch off some loose paint.

I chuckled, shaking my head.

Good lord. Some kind of handyman I am. I must have accidentally scratched this area at some point, probably with my ladder or something. Guess I was dreaming about those sounds last night.

I still had part of a can of white exterior paint left over, so I touched up over the scratches, finishing just as my three spectators started walking toward me along the driveway. It never occurred to me to bring up the scratches.

That evening, as I brought my work to a close with the sun beginning to set, the wolves started making noise again from the woods across the river.

"Do you have your hickory stick cut yet, Yank?" Earl asked.

"Nope! But I'll make one tomorrow."

"Better get it done, son. The sooner the better."

Son? Am I now son instead of Yank?

"Goodnight, Yank!" the three called out as they packed up their chairs and left.

"Apparently I'm still Yank," I sighed, chuckling as I watched the old men walk stiffly toward the road.

As it neared midnight, I couldn't seem to get comfortable enough to drift off to sleep. Tossing and turning, I tried to settle down and rest, but I just couldn't clear my mind.

A good stick of hickory. Get it done sooner than later. We're serious.

48

"Pure bullshi–"

My quiet muttering was interrupted by a sound from outside the window by my bed. Trying to figure out the sound, I leaned up on my elbow and closed my eyes to listen. It seemed like a muffled "woof," but not quite like a dog would sound.

Then I heard another sound… scratching.

It wasn't just a dream after all…

With my windows open, I decided against getting out of bed to check closer. If it was a dog or a wolf, I didn't like the idea of just a flimsy screen between me and the animal. So instead, I simply lay there listening.

After a couple of minutes, the scratching ended, and I heard no more muffled noises. I didn't move for quite some time, trying to figure out what the critter outside my window could have been.

Eventually I managed to slip off to sleep.

The next morning, I awoke with the words of the old men still echoing through my head.

"A good stick of hickory," I muttered to myself as I washed my face in the basin.

Grabbing my ax, I stepped out the door, intending to find the right stick. Adjacent to the open twenty acres upon which the schoolhouse stood, forty wooded acres sprawled out to the west, full of oak, hickory, and walnut trees. I knew I would find the right branch for what I needed in my patch of woods.

As I stepped out onto the porch, I didn't bother looking down. That morning, a beautiful sunrise catching the mist as it rose off Rockhouse Creek had my full attention. Two paces from the door, I stepped in something soft under my right boot. I looked down to discover a huge pile of shit left for me on the porch.

"Jesus, are you kidding me?" I yelled as the smell hit my nose. "What kind of monstrosity had to go that bad, and why the hell did it pick my porch?"

After carefully going down the steps on my left leg, with my right leg comically held up in the air, in hopes I wouldn't track the odiferous present all over the place, I wiped my right boot in the grass to get all the crap off the bottom, then walked over to the shed to get a shovel, muttering to myself the whole way.

"Just trying to get out this morning to get a good stick of hickory and I'm greeted by a pile of shit. By God, whoever did that must have felt better afterward. Probably was holding it in since October. October *two frickin' years ago!*"

My mutterings continued till I had the pile scooped up and dumped in the woods.

"Goddamn thing; I sure hope that's the only time – nasty shit!"

Satisfied to have the mess removed but still irritated about it, I headed into the woods to find the right hickory branch. My search didn't really take all very long, as the woods offered plenty of solid branches, most of a pretty good size. After about fifteen minutes and twenty trees, I found the hickory branch I wanted to cut: roughly two inches in diameter with the bark on and pretty straight. So, I chopped it off the tree and pulled it back to the schoolhouse.

Settling into the wooden chair I kept for porch-sitting, I sawed the stick to a four-foot length, then grabbed my old pocketknife, and began to scrape the bark away. After getting the surface fairly clean, I took one end and began to whittle, working it until I had a good point extending back about four inches to the original diameter.

"Damn varmints will feel that sticking into them," I muttered to myself, content to have only spent a couple of hours to make my wolf stick. "I still think they sound like coyotes instead of wolves."

Within an hour, my three old spectators were back with their chairs, waiting to see what I planned to tackle.

Once they were settled and ready to watch, I brought my wolf stick to them, to get their approval. Ed gave it a thorough examination.

"Not bad, Yank. You got 'er good and clean, and I like this point you put on it." He nodded as he passed the stick to Herman, who instantly poked his finger against the pointed end.

"Yeah, not bad," he said. "If you ever have to use it, you'll have to sharpen it again the next day, you know."

He nodded and passed it to Earl.

"Not bad, Yank, not bad. Bet Mrs. Briller's boy wished he had one like this that night."

"Hey, speaking of Mrs. Briller and her boy, I met Mrs. Higgins on Saturday. I guess she and Mrs. Briller are friends?" I grinned, happy to announce I met another living soul in Thermal.

"Enemies is more like it," Earl said as he continued examining the stick. "Both those women wanted to marry Briller. Joyce got 'im. Edna never forgave her."

"Edna is Mrs. Higgins' first name? She never said."

"Typical for that old witch. Stay clear of her, Yank," Ed spoke up.

"Really?" I chuckled, "I'm supposed to be afraid of a little old lady?"

"Laugh all you want, Yank. She's trouble. Some people are just… just trouble. She's one of 'em."

Earl handed the stick back to me and nodded, then took a puff off his cigar.

"Yeah, I think I managed to make her mad. I ran into her at Gibbons Store. We nearly ran over each other and she ended up dropping her bottle of milk. It went everywhere. I apologized but she shook her boney finger in my face and seemed pretty upset."

Earl scowled. "She's trouble, Yank. Just remember."

"Tell you what, fellas, speaking of trouble, I had the biggest pile of shit on my porch this morning!" I laughed after taking the stick back from Earl.

All three old men glanced quickly at each other.

"Whatever did that sure had been holding it awhile," I continued, shaking my head.

The three men just stared at me.

"Son, you better keep a close eye," Ed said, his face looking more pale than normal. "I wouldn't go out after dark and try your stick out. Not tonight. Not for a few nights."

"Several nights," Herman chimed in.

"What are you talking about?"

"That pile of shit was a sign." Ed pointed his gnarled-up finger at me. "You've been marked."

"Marked!" I laughed. "Marked by who?"

"Not who," Earl spoke up, "but *what*."

I looked at Ed then Earl and Herman.

No one said a word. I could hear my heart pounding in my ears as the three of them stared at me without saying a word.

Finally, Ed spoke up.

"There are things in these woods, Yank."

"Alright, you guys, enough trying to scare the outsider," I laughed, waving them off. "No coyote or wolf could take a dump that huge. It would have taken about six of them to have made such a big mess, trust me."

"You don't know how big it was –"

"Ed!" Herman shouted.

Ed turned to Herman and Earl. Both men glared disapprovingly at him.

"I'm just telling you, don't take a walk tonight," Ed said, lowering his head as he turned back toward me.

"You know, all this talk reminds me, something was scratching the wall outside my window last night. And it happened night before last too. I just painted over the scratches yesterday. I meant to look at the spot again today to see what the scratches look like."

Ed glanced at Herman then Earl.

"Show us," they said together as they got up from their chairs.

I took them around to the side of the house, and sure enough, there were two scratches again near my window.

I ran my fingers along the scratches as the old men watched.

After a long silence, Earl was the first to speak.

"Yank, be careful. The pile of shit and these scratches… you're marked for sure."

"Better keep a shotgun loaded." Ed shook his head.

Herman said nothing.

"Ok, guys, whatever. I've got my stick and I'll load my gun. Now, I want to get back to work on this place."

The three men walked in silence back to their chairs as I grabbed my ladder.

Nothing more was said about the wolves throughout the rest of the day. They watched as I worked, pointing out any misstep or error I made, usually within a fraction of a second of me discovering it.

The day wore into evening, and as the sun began to set, they gathered up their chairs as usual and began to leave.

"Remember what I said," Ed said as he brushed past me.

I watched them leave, shook my head, and walked inside the schoolhouse to make dinner.

At about eight o'clock, the sun was nearly set, and I wanted to take a walk. The warnings of the old men still rang in my ears, but I refused to let them stop me.

I lit my old lantern, put on my backpack, then grabbed my fine hickory stick, and set out for a walk.

When I bought the old schoolhouse property, the Realtor told me about the Old School Trail and how it meandered through the woods and covered most of the property. Back in the days of the schoolhouse actually being used for education, some area children used the trail to get there. Each surrounding homestead had its own path linking up with the trail, which made it easy for kids to get to school. As I started out into the woods along the path, I imagined all the shenanigans which could have taken place amongst the trees and overgrown brush when the kids felt ornery.

After about half an hour of walking, the woods grew substantially darker, as the sun set behind the hills to the west. I was glad to have the lantern with me to illuminate the path.

At once, I became aware of considerable yipping and howling. It sounded exactly the same as all the other nights, but closer. Much closer. The hair on the back of my neck stood up as the noise got louder. I stopped in my tracks, put my head down, closed my eyes, and listened.

That's close. Really close. Between here and the schoolhouse.

Upon opening my eyes, I became aware of the sound of leaves crunching – *many* leaves crunching – like the sound of several feet coming at me very quickly. I reached down and opened up the lantern wick a little further, splashing brighter light around me. The crunching drew near.

Suddenly, the sound grew quieter. I still heard it, as I heard nothing else. No wind, no other rustling, just the sound of those feet crunching more slowly. Slower still it approached.

Then I saw it. Then a single "it" became "them." I found myself facing eight large wolves, spread out in a line before me. Their heads were low, staring intently at me. I had seen photos and film footage of wolves before, but not like these; not this big. Easily four feet tall from paw to shoulder, these beasts were more than half my height. Their light-colored eyes, nearly white, were offset by their black fur. Seeing eight pitch-black wolves with white eyes standing in a line in front of me, I wished I had listened to my three buddies and just stayed in for the night.

I suddenly remembered a lesson from somewhere way back in my childhood.

If you ever come face-to-face with a wild animal, don't let it see you are afraid. Make yourself look large. Show no fear.

"Alright, you guys," I began to speak loudly, with as deep a voice as I could muster, "are you jackasses the ones who took a collective crap on my porch?"

The beasts didn't flinch.

Show no fear.

"Because I'd sure like to thank you for leaving me such a welcoming present! I'm still not sure it's all the way off my work boots!"

Still, the beasts didn't flinch.

Make yourself look large.

I wasn't sure where all this survival information in my head came from. But heeding the advice, I waved my arms, swinging the lantern and hickory stick, and I began to make roaring noises to the best of my ability.

The wolf in the middle began to snarl. As his nose curled back and he showed me his teeth, saliva dripped from the sides of his mouth.

"I don't think so, mister!" I yelled as I stuck my pointed hickory stick toward him.

He flinched, only a little, then looked at the other wolves. Within seconds, all eight of them snarled at me, baring their teeth.

Jesus, they are communicating.

I tried to keep from showing the fear building up inside me.

You've been marked.

The old man's words hit me like a ton of bricks. Had these little bastards come up to my porch and all eight of them taken a dump to mark where they planned to return that night?

"Alright, you little shits," I bellowed, "you may have marked my porch thinking you were coming to get me tonight, but it's not going to happen. I've got this good stick of hickory, and you're each going to feel it if you come any closer! Now get out of here! You lose!"

I did my best to come up with some guttural roar to scare them away. I took in a deep breath, leaned in toward them, and let loose a loud noise which surprised even me. With all the lung capacity I had, I let something between a growl and a roar go for ten solid seconds.

The beasts stood there looking at me as I roared. When I was done, and the last bit of air I could muster had been forced out, the middle wolf looked at me, looked at the others, and at once, they began to slowly step back away from me, facing me the entire time. After a few steps, they stopped, then sat on their haunches about twenty feet away from me.

"Ha!" I yelled after them, "That's right! You mess with me, you're messing with all kinds of trouble! Just because I'm from Michigan doesn't mean I don't know how to ward off you bastards!"

I smiled and looked down at my good stick of hickory, pleased I hadn't been forced to use it.

Just then, behind my left ear, I felt the strangest thing…

Not really a breeze but more like a hot breath which would have come from someone – or *something* – standing right behind me. As I turned around, I heard a low, deep growl.

There, standing a few inches from my face, was a beast. It stood on its hind legs, towering over me by a full twelve inches. Its feet and hands were like claws, but otherwise, it looked like a really big version of the eight wolves which were sitting and watching behind me. The beast stood before me, mouth open and dripping saliva, looking almost sadistically happy to have me at a disadvantage. After an agonizing second or two, the unbelievable happened. It spoke.

"I believe you were told to stay inside tonight, weren't you?"

I couldn't believe my ears.

As terror took a firm grip over me, I looked down at the neck of the beast. There, hanging around its neck, was a rough leather string with odd little shapes, smooth and of an off-white color.

My eyes widened as I realized who, or what, was standing in front of me.

"Mrs. Higgins?"

It laughed, a low, demonic laugh.

"Correct, Mr. Horner. You recognized my necklace! Would you like to know what these little pieces of white are on this necklace?"

Somehow in my horror I managed to nod.

"Souvenirs, Mr. Horner. Pieces of skull. You might say they are trophies."

The beast pointed at the last piece on the string.

"This was Seth Briller's. And somewhere on here is a bit of his dad's skull too. I'm just not sure now which one; there have been so many."

I looked down at the skull fragments and then back up into the beast's eyes.

"I kinda figured you would make a tasty meal for me – sooner or later. You know, you really should slow down, quit scaring little old ladies. I think you need to be taught a lesson. Who knows, I might add what's left of you to my necklace."

The beast reached up and wrapped her claw around my throat, tightening her grip as I struggled to breathe.

You might have to poke one to get it away from you.

My hickory stick, which I thankfully had not dropped in my terror, lay horizontal in my hand. Thinking quickly, I jabbed the sharp stick deep into the beast's abdomen.

It grunted then tightened its grip on my throat.

"You silly fool! Haven't you ever been told something like me can only be killed by a piece of silver? Don't you watch movies? They always use something silver, like a silver bullet."

Struggling to breathe, I managed to grin and choked out the words, "Look down."

The beast's look of anger and hate turned to shock and pain as it looked down. There, firmly strapped to my hickory stick and half buried in the beast's abdomen, was one of my mother's knives from her set of flatware – silver flatware.

Letting go of my throat, the beast stumbled backward. I drove the stick deeper into her gut as she fell to the ground.

"I'm no fool, Mrs. Higgins. I knew something wasn't right here. Tonight, I was prepared, hoping whatever was out here would take the bait."

She gasped only once.

I pulled my backpack off my shoulders. Inside, as part of my plan, I packed a can of lighter fluid and some matches. After dousing her body and all the grass about a foot around her, I struck a match and let her burn.

Turning around, I noticed the wolves were still sitting there, several feet away, looking at me and the flames. They had watched the entire scene unfold, though I must admit in the horror of the moment, I completely forgot about them.

The center wolf stepped toward me, stopping about a foot away. It then turned and looked at the other wolves, who slowly stepped forward as well, making a line like they did when they first confronted me. Unsure of what would happen next, I held my ground.

Together, the wolves lowered their heads, as if to acknowledge me and what I did, then raised them again and stared at me. I nodded slowly in return. Then mustering up my courage, I knelt down in front of them. One by one, they came forward and nudged my shoulder with the tops of their heads, then ran off toward Rockhouse Creek Hollow, howling and yipping the entire way.

I turned back around as what was left of Mrs. Higgins continued to burn with the silver knife and the singed remains of my hickory stick conspicuously sticking up.

From that point on, I was no longer afraid to take walks near dusk, or of any sounds I heard outside my window.

The wolves now answered to me.

SPOILING THE BELLS

———————— •●• ————————

The following is an extract from the interview with Ronald Eugene Warren, dated March 4, 1891, at the Commercial Street Police Station in Shoreditch, in the East End of London. The interview was conducted by investigating officer William L. Breach, whose comments and questions are herein omitted for clarity, and to allow Mr. Warren's statements to be the sole voice within this narrative. The complete transcripts are located within the National Archives, London.

My name is Ronald Eugene Warren, and I was born June 6, 1861, in Philadelphia, Pennsylvania, in America. My father joined the 75th Regiment, Pennsylvania Infantry, after my birth and was killed on the second day of the Battle of Gettysburg. My mother died in 1868 during the smallpox outbreak. I have no siblings, so our neighbors, Mr. and Mrs. Etheridge, raised me once my mother fell ill.

At the age of 16, I entered an apprenticeship at the Stow Foundry on Second Street in Philadelphia. Mr. John Stow died many decades prior, but his successor elected to keep the Stow name due to its popularity and recognition. After four years of apprenticeship, I was assigned Keeper of the Furnace. That position has the responsibility for not only maintaining the fires below the pour cauldrons, for consistent temperatures, but also has the duty of removing ash and other byproducts of combustion on a regular basis. Shortly after achieving Keeper of the Furnace, I decided to continue my apprenticeship for an additional two years so I might earn the position of Pour Master, which I know you call Pour Guard here in England.

The duty of the Pour Master or Pour Guard is to maintain proper flow during the transfer of the liquified metal into the mold. Additionally, prior to the pour, it is my responsibility to watch the open area above the large cauldron, to prevent any foreign object from falling into the molten material. A foreign object falling into the molten alloy pollutes the material and results in a poor-quality casting. "Spoiling the Bells" we call it, and that's a general term whether we are casting a bell or some other type of large piece.

I was named Pour Master at age 22, and within one year resigned to take a position as Pour Guard at the White Chapel Bell Foundry here in the East End. I left the American harbor aboard the steamer SS Philadelphia on May 3, 1884, and arrived in London on May 12, as our normal 6-day crossing was slowed by a storm. You are welcome to check the ship's manifest to verify this information.

I was motivated to relocate to London because my grandfather, Elias Warren, was born here, and I have an uncle still residing within the city who invited me to come to work at the foundry. His flat is here in the East End, at 47 Middlesex Street. His name is Nathaniel Jackson Warren, also employed at the foundry. Any neighbor in the block can verify I have been lodging with him these nearly seven years since arriving.

My shift at the foundry begins at 2:00a.m. each day. I typically leave my uncle's flat at 1:30 and make my way along Middlesex Street then turn onto White Chapel Road. It is then just a few blocks to the foundry. I work until 6:00 p.m. except on Sundays; on such day, I leave at 11:30 a.m to attend the noon mass, and then I have the rest of the day off.

We have a six-man crew in the pouring area: William

Edgewater is the Mold Guard and starts his shift at 2:00 a.m. with me. Then Thomas LaGrue, Jonathan Beales, Edward Beales, Jonathan's younger brother, and David Petlovski round out the crew as utility workers and general helpers. They normally start their shift at 3:00 a.m.

I tell you all of this with the understanding you are most welcome to check the facts on any or all details I have just told you. I want you to have no doubt I am telling you the truth, as everything else I am about to say has great bearing on your present investigation.

I first met Francis Coles in December of 1889. I regret I cannot give you the precise date, but we met at Christ Church Spitalfields at a Sunday evening public reading of *A Christmas Carol*, you know, the story by Charles Dickens. They've been doing public readings of the story there for over fifty years now, and though I've heard the story many times, I still enjoy listening to it being read at the church each Christmastime.

That evening, the reading event was so popular with the locals, there was nowhere left to sit by the time I arrived. While standing in the back of the room, I began to scan the crowd, and I caught the glance of Francis. I noticed she was dressed poorly, but her smile and kind brown eyes caught my attention. I found her to be most pleasant and attractive. I remember when our eyes met and we exchanged smiles, I couldn't help but think "I bet her skin is soft."

After the reading, I mustered up my courage and walked over to her to introduce myself. After a short visit, she accepted my invitation to stroll in the chilly evening. We walked and visited for several blocks and had a genuinely nice time together. Afterward, I met up with her as often as possible and made it known I wished to court her.

She told me she worked as a corker at the pharmacy over on Osborn Street, which was quite near the foundry.

Yes, I knew she was a part-time prostitute as well. Bleeding Christ, man, most women here end up prostituting at some point just to afford a place to stay for the night when things turn badly in their lives. It didn't change how I felt about her. She had the kindest face, and I swam in her brown eyes. Her voice had a certain lilt to it, and I loved to hear her talk. We visited for hours whenever possible and found so many similarities between us. I was truly smitten.

I was unable to tolerate her when she drank, though, which became more and more often. I am not taken to consuming spirits myself. Her drinking worsened, so I stopped seeing her last summer. By then, she was living in Spitalfields Chambers, drank entirely too often, and prostituted nearly full-time to pay for lodging and food. It pained me to break away from her, but I couldn't continue courting her if she was to live such a life.

We encountered each other again at, of all places, Christ Church Spitalfields. She still looked poor and had been prostituting, but all those old feelings reached the surface again, and we spent nearly two hours talking within the confines of the church.

She knew about the unsolved murders in the White Chapel region, and admitted she was uncomfortable about being out on the streets after dark. I gave her some money during our visit that night. It wasn't much, just the few pounds I happened to be carrying. As we bid each other goodnight and walked away in opposite directions, I felt sadly certain the money I gave her for lodging would be used up by the consuming of various spirits.

Yes, the guys on my crew at the foundry knew how I felt about Francis. They teased me about having feelings for a woman known to prostitute, and said things like, "Who do you think she's with this morning, Ronny?" David Petlovski was especially persistent with harsh comments, and he liked keeping all of us abreast of the developments in the neighborhood murders and what he knew about the latest victims.

All that time, I worried about poor Francis. Word got to me she had taken up with a man called James Sadler and they were living together but combative with one another, especially when drinking.

We heard about the murder of Mary Kelly on November 9 three years ago. While all of us were taking our noon meal, David stepped out to buy some tobacco. He came back breathless, telling us of the heinous killing and the dreadful condition in which the woman was found, saying the neighborhood was filled with people talking about it. The killing took place just a couple of blocks away from the flat I share with my uncle.

A few days later, while our crew was working, the subject of Mary's murder was mentioned, I think by Thomas LaGrue, and David spoke up.

"I attended the coroner's inquest, you know," he bragged.

"Now why in the name of everything holy would you do that?" asked Edward loudly. All of us nearly yelled when we had a conversation, to be heard over the furnace.

"Because I wanted to see if what they wrote in the papers about the body was true."

"Well, was it?" Jonathan asked as he helped his brother set the cope onto the lower bell form.

"It was the most horrific sight I have ever laid eyes upon, lads. She didn't look human. It was as if she was ripped apart by a big dog, one of those big mountain dogs I've heard tell of. Mark my words, mates, this man, this Jack, or whoever he is, he's a devil, a beast, not a man."

LaGrue grunted, never looking up from his crouched position as he held the lower mold.

I have to admit, sometimes the actions and demeanor of my coworkers made me wonder at times if the murderer was really one of them.

Two mornings ago, I arrived at work around 1:45 and

changed into my work clothes as I normally do. William usually gets there at about the same time as I, and we typically have a chat before starting work. We are always the only ones in the entire facility at that time of morning. He had not yet arrived, so I dressed alone. While putting on my apron, I heard the main door open. Thinking it was William, I called out but received no answer. I didn't hear any footsteps either, which I thought was odd. Out of necessity when pouring molten metal at nearly 600 degrees, we all wear heavy leather boots. One would have to be a fool to wear anything softer. Since we all wear such boots, anyone walking around can be heard quite distinctly. Yet at this moment, I heard nothing.

I began to worry a prowler may have entered the building. I quickly removed my boots and walked to the door leading from our pouring room to the machining section, where extra bits from the casting process are cut away from the workpiece. Through the dirty window on the door, I saw a woman in shabby clothes walking quickly. She walked stooped over and appeared to be holding something as she moved. She walked to the office of the superintendent, but it is always locked at such an early hour, so entry was denied her.

I slipped through the door and made certain it closed quietly behind me, and I pursued her as she moved to the next office, home of the tool master. He apparently failed to lock his door upon leaving the previous day, as I saw the lady slip in and close the door behind her. She appeared to be wearing some type of soft-soled shoe, which I caught sight of as she walked. That explained why I never heard her walking into the building.

I made up my mind she must have been one of the prostitutes in the area, and she came to steal tools in hopes of making a bit of money from them. Our tools are of precise dimension and great material strength, therefore are worth considerable money, and their replacement costs are high. I was not about to allow her to steal from my employer.

When I got to the tool master's office, I heard rustling inside. Grasping the doorknob and turning it as quietly as possible, in hopes of surprising the woman, I threw open the door and let out a yell, which did indeed surprise the woman. She let out the oddest shriek and turned to face me.

I could not believe my eyes as I looked upon this woman. She was drenched with a red liquid which I supposed to be blood, from her face all the way down the front of her dress. Her eyes were wide from being discovered, and she held a large knife in her hands, which also displayed the crimson liquid. But the thing about her which surprised me the most was her face. That's because she was clearly a man. And not just any man.

I looked at him in his bloody dress with the knife in his hand and yelled, "Uncle Nathaniel! What the hell?"

In an instant, his face went from frightened to angry, and he scowled at me.

"Dammit, Ronny! You didn't give me time to change!"

He glared at me but neither of us moved. I was in such a state of shock, looking at my uncle standing there in a bloody dress, with a wig on and holding a knife covered in crimson.

"Uncle Nathaniel... what... what have you done?"

"Oh, Ronny boy, tonight, I did yet again what I've been doing for some time. Clearing the streets, you might say."

"Clearing the str..." I stammered as my thoughts collided. "Uncle – you mean – are you telling me – you're – you're the man they call Jack The Ripper?"

He leered at me, blood still running down his clothes.

"Oh, I couldn't help giving myself that name. The papers loved it. And I thought it clever, signing the letter with my middle name – eh, Nephew?"

I suddenly remembered the letter published in the

newspaper back in '88, signed by "Jack the Ripper." Uncle Nathaniel's middle name, as I noted before, was Jackson.

My uncle watched as all of it became clear in my head. He then pointed the knife toward me.

"So... now you know... that means you gotta be next, Nephew. Nothing personal..." He gave me an awful, evil grin as he said it.

"Why should I be next?" I asked, trying to stall for time.

"Well, you know, so many women, so many fallen angels, have laid prey to my knife..."

He held it up, looking at it. Then he returned his gaze to me.

"You might talk. You might tell someone what you've seen. I never planned to kill a man. But plans change."

I couldn't move. I wanted to run but my legs weren't listening.

"Like I said, nothing personal, mate."

He lunged at me.

I had to think quickly.

Still holding the door, I jumped up and gave him a kick in the face. I heard a distinct snap as the impact broke his nose, sending him to the floor as everything began to move in slow motion.

As he rolled over, clutching his face, I turned and ran out the door, making a quick dash to the pouring room. I slammed the door behind me, never bothering to look back over my shoulder to see how close he was. Running into the middle of the room, I looked for somewhere to hide. Seeing nothing safe, I instinctively climbed up to the top of the deslagging platform. That's the metal grate over the cauldron, where I typically stand to remove slag floating at the top of the molten metal before pouring. I wanted to get up high, in hopes of having an upper hand.

My uncle burst into the room just as I made it up to the platform.

"You can't get away, you know." He stared up at me, blood streaming down his face.

I wanted to stall for more time.

"Uncle, I don't understand. Why the women's clothing? And what happened tonight? What did you do?"

He grinned.

"The police, they be looking for a man. They be listening for his footsteps. If I dress like a woman, they do not suspect me, even as I walk by them. I wear soft-soled ladies' shoes, so there are no footsteps to hear."

He began scaling the steps to the top of the platform where I was standing.

"You saw the blood on my dress. I've brought in lots of bloody dresses. But all of them have found their way into the furnace after you started it burning."

"You – you were here each time after you killed those women?" I was stunned. I never heard nor saw him.

"Yes. I began coming here early to study your patterns. Did you know after you ignite the furnace, you always leave for 45 seconds? And did you know your shoes are so loud I can clearly hear them as you return?"

"I didn't know. So that's how you got rid of the bloody evidence each time?"

"Yes." He nodded as he continued to move closer, the knife in his hand pointed at me. "And each time, the knife melted away in the cauldron."

"Very clever, Uncle." I shook my head. "I never knew a thing. So, your target tonight – do you have any idea who she was?"

"Oh yes." He grinned. "And so did you."

"What do you mean?"

He looked down at his knife then looked back at me.

"How long has it been since you last saw Francis?"

A wave of horror shot through me.

"No!"

"Yes! Your little drunk whore, spending all her time

with another man, looked very different when I left her room a short time ago. Very different indeed." He snickered as he stared at me.

I drew both hands into a tight fist.

"As a matter of fact," he laughed, "I don't think you would recognize her pretty little face at all."

He had killed my Francis. Yes, I knew she wasn't really mine and she had taken up with another man. But I always hoped maybe, someday, she might come back, and I could give her a different life.

My mind raced, my heart began to thump hard in my chest, and for a moment, I saw nothing but red.

Then with a yell, I lunged at him.

In that tiny second, I tried to knock his hand holding the knife, so I could hit him. But he jumped out of the way, and as I moved past him, he brought the knife down, tearing a gash in my right arm.

Despite the pain, I spun around and tried to get at him again. Catching him slightly off-balance, I hit him from his right side and knocked him onto the grated surface of the platform. I tried to get to his knife, but he began slashing wildly, cutting me in the arm again and on my face. I punched him hard, knocking his head against the grate. Filled with rage, he shoved me off him.

I got to my feet quickly as he rose to face me.

We stood there, staring as we crouched toward one another, he holding the knife as I felt the blood running down my face and arm.

He then jumped at me. With my left arm, I tried to knock his right knife-wielding hand away from me, but as I did, he swung with his left arm and buried his fist in my gut. I let out a yell and doubled over as he brought his knee up into my face. That's what caused all this swelling and blackened eyes you see on me.

I lost the ability to defend myself at that moment, and sunk to my knees, leaning forward as I began to cough up blood.

Uncle Nathan leaned down next to me.

"You fool! Just what the bloody hell did you think you were doing, hanging around on the streets – in public! Being seen with that whore."

He stood up and kicked me hard in the stomach. I groaned and rolled over onto the grate.

He knelt down next to me again.

"You brought shame to this family, Ronny. The neighbors talked when they saw you walking with Francis. I couldn't let you shame our family name anymore. I would have been perfectly happy to just kill her to make this stop. But now, since you know about what I've been doing, the important service I've been offering to the people of this area... well, you know, I can't let you walk around with such knowledge."

He rolled me over onto my back.

"Don't worry, Nephew, no one will find you."

He looked below at the glowing cauldron filled with molten copper for the morning's bell pour.

"You can become an integral part of this morning's casting."

In that moment, mixed with the pain from my wounds, so many emotions blasted through me. I was furious to know the murderous beast who had fooled the police for so long was my own filthy uncle. It broke my heart to know I could never again look into the loving eyes of Francis and hope for a better future for the two of us. I was enraged to find myself in a life-or-death struggle with the man they called The Ripper, a man who managed to execute his capers by cowardly dressing up as a woman.

While doubled over after he kicked me, I noticed the slag scoop was within reach. It was a six-foot-long rod with an elongated cup on the end. Made of one inch round steel, the handle was strong enough to withstand the heat.

Just then, we heard a door slam closed. Dropping his

guard, my uncle turned and looked toward the sound.

I knew my chance had come. Mustering up all the strength I could, I reached over and grabbed the scoop and swung it as hard as I could. The rod hit my uncle in the side of his knee. His leg bent to the side as he screamed. He toppled over, landing on his side.

I struggled to my feet. Standing over him, I swung again and again, bringing the now-bloody rod down on his head, then moved down to hit him in his side.

Knowing he was all but incapacitated, I caught my breath. The beast, the devil incarnate, The Ripper, lay gasping and bleeding at my feet. In a moment, I knew what I had to do.

I rolled him over. He looked up at me through the blood covering his face.

"Wha- what are you going to do now, Nephew?" he gasped. "The police will hang me."

My face and arm were still bleeding but I no longer felt anything.

"Hanging isn't enough punishment for you... Uncle!" I sneered.

I leaned down behind him and rolled him over – toward the edge where I normally stood to skim the slag off the cauldron.

Realizing what I was doing, he let out a cry.

"No! No, Ronny! Don't burn me!"

He began to sob.

"Are you crying, Uncle?" I mocked him. "Did Francis cry when she realized the bastard she was facing? Did all those women cry? Or did you just take life from them before they could?"

"You – you're not supposed to be the one who passes judgement!" He pleaded. It made me sick to listen to him.

"Oh really! Do tell!" I sneered as I rolled him closer to the edge.

"It – it says – it says so in the Bible you know."

I was almost amused to hear Jack the Ripper tell me something about the Bible. I had heard enough.

I rolled him to the edge of the grate, face down, so he could see the boiling copper below him.

"I don't think the Bible is going to have any bearing on where you're going!"

I gave him a hard push, and he yelled "No!" as he tumbled over the edge and into the cauldron. He hit with a splash, sending fat bits of metal flying in all directions.

As the pieces of glowing copper alloy landed all over the room, William Edgewater walked in, ready to start our day's shift. I looked down at the cauldron, to see if anything moved within the liquid.

Nothing.

"What in the name of Bleeding Christ happened here?" William yelled, looking around then seeing me standing there atop the platform, bleeding from my various wounds.

I wiped my face with my sleeve, spat blood into the cauldron, then turned to him and said, "The bells are going to be spoiled today."

MEMORIAL NIGHT

A heavy mist falls thick below the bluffs
As the wind blows, screaming past my ears,
Chilling me to the point of pain.
'Tis punishment for my late-night journey.

I pull my frock around me,
Fancying it provides full protection
From unknowns which lie in wait –
But alas wool can only protect me from the cold,

Nothing else.

The road looks much different by day,
Always a bit steep and rocky;
But now the lane feels so dark and deadly,
Full of night's creatures.

My lantern, fighting to stay alit,
Captures pairs of eyes, low to the ground,
Watching me. Following me.
From a distance they seem safe.

Even creatures lurking about in the dark
Seem frightened this night.

I struggle to find sure footing
As I continue my trek upward
To the familiar stone entrance,
Now coming into view.

Stopping at the worn wrought iron gate,
I neaten the fragrant bouquet
Brought to this horrifying place of Rest
With my dearest in mind
In loving hope it may keep her warm.

I work my way to the familiar stone,
Though tonight's godless black
Casts Hell's darkest shadow
Over even her grave.

Dropping to my knees,
I lean toward the cold granite,
Damp to the touch,
To sweep the wet leaves away
From her precious name.

"Lysette," I whisper
As I place my gift on the earth,
"Your love has returned to bid you well –
I hope you are comfortable."

Another gale comes screaming through the valley
As twigs snap behind me.

Is someone there?

The flame in my lantern surrenders to the wet gust,
Extinguished forever,
And I panic
As I am plunged into darkness.

Yet I know where I am,
My love lies beneath the very soil
I now kneel upon.

Overcome with emotion,
I grieve, cry aloud, and ask the moonless sky,
"Why?!"

I must kiss the soil entombing her delicate form,
As tears roll down my face
And drip onto the earth below me.

My pulse quickens, my mind races, my body trembles
As in darkness I slowly lean toward the ground.

What madness is this? Am I dreaming?
As my lips, cold and wet, touch the mossy ground
My Lysette's face breaks through the earth
And our lips meet in a timeless kiss.

I blink quickly, lest my sleep continue
And this dream, this nightmare takes me.
Yet I am awake.
I realize to my horror
The nightmare is real!

Her cold, gray, wet hands and legs
Quickly break through the mound.
Around my neck her fingers crawl.
Her lengthy nails penetrate my skin
As her icy grip suddenly tightens.

Pull away I try. I cannot move!
My love, my sweet Lysette, undead,
Has me.

My eyes gaze upon Lysette's lifeless stare
As her teeth latch onto my bloodied lower lip.
My muscles strain, fighting against her pull
As tightly her legs wrap around me.

To scream I try, though who can come?
I am alone, with no one near this place
For many miles.
I am alone.

I must escape! I must break free!
Yet my every exertion is met with agony
As my love, my undead love,
Drives her nails deeper into my skin.

My futile resistance ends as my joints collapse
While she continues our painful kiss
And I let out a muffled cry as I'm slowly pulled down
To forever join my lovely Lysette.

THE OLD 592

Brothers and sisters, mind my words, and heed this
scary tale of mine.
Run, hide, and cover your ears when you hear the
whistle of the old Chadwick Line;
For the iron beast is done, it breathes no more, and the
tracks have long gone away.
But some dark nights when there is no moon, the old
train comes back to life, they say.
Do not try to see the old locomotive, and stay away from
the ghoulish track,
For all those who've boarded the Chad Ghost Train
have never, ever come back.

Ozarks Folk Legend

"All that ghost train stuff is a bunch of crap."
Lee Walker stayed quiet as his friend Jesse
Trowbridge continued to debunk the old legend while they
walked home from Sparta High School. A warm spring
wind whipped up dust around them as they made their way
along the gravel road.

"Listen, Lee, the tracks for the real train were pulled
up between Ozark and Chadwick in the early 1930s. The
depot here in town was moved, and Old Man Matthews
even plowed up the roadbed in his field so he could go back
to growing corn. So how exactly do you suppose it can
make its way here with no tracks and no water for the
steam engine?"

"It's a ghost train, Jesse. Don't need no tracks or water." Lee didn't look at Jesse as he spoke. He just looked straight ahead.

"That's bullshit and you know it," Jesse snapped back. "Good lord, Lee, it's 1955. We're past old legends about such things. It's just not possible."

"All I know is, I heard a train whistle one night last month. It was one of those nights without no moon, and it was foggy because we had a bunch of rain, and I heard a whistle. It didn't come from a train in Ozark. And there's no other trains within earshot of this area. Whatever made that whistle sound came straight through Sparta, right along the path of the old train."

The two boys stopped and looked at each other.

"Think what you will, Jesse. I know what I heard."

Jesse shook his head and grinned.

"Well, if you're going to believe that old train, that *ghost train*, is for real, then you better pay attention to the rest of the legend. Don't try to get on or you'll never come back."

"I don't know about getting on it; I just want to see it."

"Does your daddy know you think you've heard it?"

"No. But Dad is the one who told me about the legend. He heard the whistle when he was a boy, about ten years after the train stopped running. But he doesn't know I've heard it."

"Probably better not tell him."

"No, probably not."

They stood in silence for a moment. They had reached the crossing of Bull Creek and Shawnee roads. Lee lived in the old farmhouse on the corner, while Jesse lived farther down Bull Creek Road.

"You know, Jesse," Lee eventually spoke up, "you ought to consider planning to come over and spend the night at our house whenever the next new moon hits this summer. We could stay up and listen for the whistle.

There's still an extra cot in my room from when Grandpa visited last."

"New moon is supposed to be just this coming Friday night. I bet my folks would let me."

"Alright, then. Work it out with them and I'll tell my folks."

Jesse walked on toward home as Lee turned and went inside his house.

That Friday night, Jesse brought a few clothes and his ball glove with him and had dinner at the Walker house. Afterward, the boys played catch in the front yard till well after dark, till they couldn't see the ball anymore to catch it. Then they made their way to Lee's room to listen for the whistle. The night was warm, warmer than usual for May, so Lee opened his window to help them listen.

After about an hour of listening, Jesse couldn't stand the silence any longer and had to say something.

"Do you hear anything, Lee?"

Lee shook his head.

"Not a thing. Not yet at least."

"Is this thing supposed to appear at midnight or something? I've heard that's considered the witching hour."

"Well." Lee turned to Jesse. "I hate to argue about such things, but I think you heard wrong. According to my grandfather, the witching hour is supposed to be between three and four in the morning. It's supposed to be when the veil between the living and the dead is thinnest. Midnight is just midnight."

"Ok, so was it three o'clock when you think you heard the whistle?"

"I don't know what time it was. Wasn't no clock in the room."

Then the boys heard a noise. It sounded like a low rumble.

"What's that? Sounded like a rumble. Does the train rumble when it shows up? Maybe it's coming but hasn't sounded the whistle yet."

"I don't recall hearing a rumble that night," Lee whispered. "I just recall hearing the whistle."

Then suddenly they saw a flash of light, followed by another rumble.

Lee let out a sigh, turned away from the window, and slid down onto his bed.

"That's not the train. It's a thunderstorm coming. The ghost train is not going to show up during a thunderstorm. Not going to happen tonight, Jesse."

Jesse sighed, closed the window, and settled down onto the spare cot to go to sleep.

"There'll be a new moon next month, Lee. We can try again."

"Yep."

Lee rolled over and went to sleep as the thunderstorm drew closer and got louder.

The following Monday afternoon, the boys started their walk home from school with plenty to discuss.

"I dug a bit more into the history of your 'spooky' Chadwick train thing," Jesse said, unfolding a sheet of paper he dug out of his pocket. "Turns out, it ran for about fifty years, was never on time, and people around here loved it."

"That's pretty much what I've heard," Lee said without looking at Jesse.

"Yeah, but there's a lot more. It had a six-man crew, with a guy by the name of Lyons as the engineer. Charlie McBride was a brakeman and allegedly everyone knew him, and he knew everybody. For a big part of its history, the train was often a mixed run, so it had passenger cars and freight cars. The locomotive was numbered 592, and it ran from Springfield to Chadwick and back seven days a week."

"Seven days a week? No weekends off?" Lee scowled.

"According to our neighbor!"

"Your neighbor?"

"Yeah, Old Man Bradley. He knows a lot of history around here."

"So how did this thing turn around at Chadwick to go back to Springfield?"

"Get this." Jesse started talking faster in his excitement, reading from his notes. "They built a wooden turntable in Chadwick. The locomotive and tinder were separated from the cars, went down a hill, and under a full head of steam, the whole thing was spun around by hand."

"They operated the turntable manually?"

"Yep, sure did. Then it steamed back up the hill, latched on to the rear car, and was ready to head back to Springfield."

"I've been to Chadwick a million times" – Lee turned to Jesse – "and there's no turntable there."

"Nope. It only lasted a few years then they replaced it with a wye in the tracks. It was a lot easier, just switching tracks a couple of times to get the locomotive and tinder turned around."

"Makes sense," Lee said as they neared his house.

The two boys stopped at the corner, before Jesse had to keep going to his house.

"Look, you've got me all riled up to see this thing too." Jesse grinned. "So, let's figure out how to make it happen."

Lee thought for a minute.

"Well, we've already decided you're coming over whenever there is a new moon. I've looked it up in the almanac, it's the night of June 18th. That's a Saturday night. So, you come over, and I'd say we make sure we secretly pack a flashlight and some provisions. We'll just have to be ready to jump if we hear the whistle."

"You mean *when* we hear it!" Jesse chuckled.

"Yeah. *When.*" Lee grinned.

The night of June 18th came and went, and the boys spent the night together, listening for the whistle but were disappointed. They set their sights on the next night with a new moon, July 17th.

July in Sparta was always hot, humid, and dusty. Lee and Jesse spent their days drenched with sweat while they worked on the loading dock of the local feed store. An occasional afternoon thundershower was a welcome respite, though in the aftermath, the humidity and temperature rose again. The evenings were just as hot and humid, and the night of the seventeenth, as the boys lay in Lee's room listening and waiting, a small fan whirred quietly, stirring the air to make the summer night a bit more bearable. Then in the quiet stillness, Lee heard his mother's wind chimes begin to tinkle, ever so quietly. He got up out of bed and peered out the window into the night to feel whatever breeze had come by.

Lee's window faced west, and as he looked out the window, his eyes detected some sort of movement in the distance.

"Jesse, are you awake? I see something. Get over here."

Jesse jumped out of bed and stuck his head out the window next to Lee.

At first, it looked like a plume of smoke. Then it spread out into the countryside, like fog.

"Do you see that?" Lee whispered.

"Yes. I see something vertical, like smoke. Like it's coming out of a smokestack."

"Yeah but look at what's down at the ground level too. It's like a mist or fog or something."

Then they heard it. A steam whistle. Like the ones on locomotives.

"Holy shit, Jesse, that's it! The ghost train!"

"Do I see a light coming?"

"Yes! Let's go!"

Quickly but quietly, the boys grabbed their satchel with the flashlight and provisions and ran toward town on

Bull Creek Road. In a matter of moments, they reached the tracks. Looking west toward the site of the old depot, they were stunned. There, surrounded in fog and mist, belching steam from its stack, with headlight glowing brightly, was a train.

Walking slowly toward it, the boys finally began to speak.

"There's two passenger cars attached to it," Jesse whispered.

"Yeah."

The locomotive continued to puff steam as it sat, like it was breathing, waiting.

"Jesse, look." Lee stopped and grabbed Jesse by the arm, then pointed at the front of the train. Jesse looked then the boys glanced at each other. The locomotive was Number 592.

Lee quickened his pace. They got within about one hundred feet of the train, then Jesse stopped.

"Lee, what if it's, you know, cursed, like the legend says? What if we can't get off once we get on?"

Lee looked at Jesse.

"I reckon that's why we ran all this way. To find out if it's true."

They looked at each other, nodded, then walked to the train. They looked up into the darkened cab of the locomotive. Two eyes peered back at them from the blackness.

A man in a suit stepped down from the first passenger car. His cheeks were hollow, and his eyes were black, unreflective, with no life in them. Only his smile gave a hint of life in him.

"Been waitin' for you boys." The man nodded and waved them in. "Come on, Lee. Come on, Jesse. Watch your step."

The boys nodded back at the man as they climbed aboard. It took a moment for their eyes to adjust to the dimly lit car. They looked around and noticed other men and women in the car, each appearing to be asleep, with their heads down.

Lee and Jesse sat down in seats beside each other just as the locomotive blew its whistle and lurched forward.

"All aboard," Jesse muttered.

"What did you say?" Lee turned to Jesse.

"All aboard. He never said, 'all aboard.'"

"Well, you heard how he greeted us by name. It's as if they were expecting us. Maybe only us."

The train began to gain speed as it traveled through Sparta then curved back south at Shipman Hill. Faster and faster, it clicked along invisible tracks toward Chadwick.

"I thought you said this thing only traveled about 12 miles per hour," Lee said, turning to Jesse.

"That's what I was told. But this sure as hell is faster."

"He will have to slow down at some point to stop at Chadwick."

"Maybe we can jump back off when he stops."

Lee turned and looked around the car at the sleeping souls. Scowling, he turned back around.

"If he doesn't slow this thing down, he's going to crash at Chadwick. There's nothing but trees after the end of the line there."

"Doesn't make sense, does it," Jesse said, shaking his head.

Suddenly they saw the shapes of several buildings as they flew by them.

"Shit, we're in Chadwick right now! Hang on, we're going to crash!" Lee yelled as he gripped the back of the seat in front of him.

The boys closed their eyes and held on.

The train, however, continued on.

"What the hell are we doing?" Lee looked around. "Why didn't we stop – or crash?"

"Oh no." Jesse laid his head down on the back of his

hands, which were still tightly gripping the back of the seat in front of him.

"'Oh no' what?" Lee frowned.

"Little Rock."

"'Little Rock' what?"

"According to what I read, this line was always meant to go all the way to Little Rock. That was the original plan. It was never meant to stop in Chadwick. At some point, the railroad decided to abandon the idea of running it all the way south and let it stop at Chadwick. We haven't stopped because this train is running along the intended route. We're going to Little Rock."

Just then, the ghoulish conductor appeared at the door. Still sporting the same grin, he walked toward the boys.

"Just guessing – he's not McBride, is he?" Jesse whispered.

"I'm sure he's not."

"And again, just guessing – those eyes looking back at us from the cab, that wasn't Lyons, the original engineer, was it?"

"Doubtful."

The man leaned down into their faces. His wide smile showed gray rotted teeth and a black mouth.

"Having a nice trip, boys?"

"Yes, sir," they said quietly.

As the ghoul started to walk away, Jesse spoke up.

"Please, sir, can you tell me what time we make it to Little Rock?"

The man turned back around and placed an icy hand on Jesse's shoulder.

"Little Rock? We don't stop in Little Rock, son. As a matter of fact, we don't stop anywhere. So just enjoy the ride!"

He laughed and patted Jesse on the shoulder then walked toward the back of the car and disappeared.

"Give me something to eat." Lee held out his hand.

"What? Didn't you hear what he just said? We're not stopping anywhere. How can you eat?"

"I need to think, and I'm hungry. Now give me something out of that bag and let me think."

Jesse dug around in the bag and brought out one of Lee's mother's biscuits the boys had smuggled back to their room to include in their provisions. Lee took it and began to eat, nodding his head as he thought. After finishing the biscuit, he began to speak softly.

"We know this guy's statement of not stopping anywhere is bullshit, because they stopped to pick us up. So, all we have to do is wait for them to stop to pick someone up and then we will jump off. Simple stuff."

"That almost sounds too simple," Jesse protested.

"You're right. I do see one problem with the plan already."

"What is it?" Jesse asked while rummaging around for another biscuit.

"We heard this train only on a moonless night. It's another month before the next new moon. Does that mean we will be on this train for a month before they stop to pick someone else up?"

"I don't like the sound of that."

"Me neither."

Lee looked around at the other seemingly lifeless people in the train car. None of them were sitting together, and each one sat in the same position: sitting up straight but with their heads down against their chests. Most were men. Some gray-headed, others bald, and others with a full head of dark hair. Only two were female: one appeared to be a middle-aged lady, and the other was seemingly young, with long brown hair covering her face.

Slowly, Lee walked back to the girl's row and sat down beside her, taking quick stock of her appearance. Her jeans were old and worn, and were a bit too short, as he could see her ankles and torn shoes. She wore a plain blouse, which also looked plenty worn. She looked like any other hardworking farm girl with whom he was acquainted in Christian County.

"Hey," he said softly. "Are you – are you in there?"

It felt like a dumb thing to say, but it was the only thing he could come up with.

The girl jumped for a moment, startled by someone speaking to her. As she turned to look at Lee next to her, she pulled her hair back from her face.

As soon as he saw her, Lee's eyes widened.

"I know you! Aren't you Penny Hobner, from Oldfield?"

The girl smiled faintly and nodded, her eyes still sad.

"We met at a church camp a few years ago, by the old cemetery on Sawmill Hollow Road! I'm Lee Walker. Do you remember?"

The girl scowled as she studied his face. Then the scowl left her face. Her eyes widened, and she smiled, then threw her arms around Lee. "Yes, it's me, Penny. I do remember you, Lee! We – we took some walks together, just you and me through those woods there. I remember!"

"I remember when you disappeared two years ago, Penny. It was in all the papers, including Springfield. You just vanished. I'm guessing you heard the whistle and got on this train?"

Penny pulled away and faced Lee.

"Yes. I couldn't help myself. I had heard the stories. I wanted to see for myself. And then when the conductor called me by name, I just couldn't – couldn't stop. I had to climb on board."

Then she stopped and looked down.

"Did you say two years? Has it been that long?"

"Yes, two years ago next month." Lee put his arm around Penny.

"My poor mom and dad. This must have just killed

them."

"It's been awful hard on them for sure. But they're both still alive and carrying on with their lives, from what I hear tell."

"I so wish I could get off of this train." Penny put her face in her hands and began to cry.

Lee pulled her in close to him.

"Penny, I got on here with my buddy Jesse. We're going to figure out how to get off of here, and when we do, we'll take you with us."

"I don't know how you'll do that. This thing never stops."

"Well, it stopped for us to get on board. There's gotta be a way."

Lee whistled to get Jesse's attention. When Jesse turned around, Lee waved him back to their seat. The bench seat opposite Lee and Penny faced them, so Jesse sat down and leaned in as Lee and Penny leaned in to talk. Lee introduced Penny to Jesse. He recognized her too.

"We gotta figure out a way to get off this train," Jesse said quietly.

"I can tell you already the windows don't open," Penny said. "I already tried them."

"Penny, does the conductor stay up there at that door to the outside, the one we boarded through?" Lee asked.

"Yes." Penny nodded. "But he's not always at the door. Sometimes he hides in a little cubby hole opposite. Then he comes walking through here once in a while."

"What about the door behind you, the one leading to the next car?" Jesse nodded toward the door behind Penny and Lee. "Does it open? Can we get to the next car back?"

"Or better yet," Lee said, "is there space between the cars where we can jump off?"

"The door will lead to the next car, yes," Penny answered. "But you can't jump from between the cars. There's some sort of solid black space between the cars.

It's not open to the air."

"Is there a caboose on this train?" Jesse asked.

"No. No caboose. And the door on the opposite end of the car doesn't open. I tried it too when I first realized I was trapped on this thing."

"Are there more people in the next car?" Lee asked.

"No, it's empty." Penny shrugged. "I'm guessing they are saving it for when this car gets too full."

"Well, how 'bout we go back there," Lee said, "We'll get a little farther away from the conductor and see if we can figure out something."

The trio stood up together and turned to see if the conductor was nearby. There was no sign of him, so they quietly made their way to the door, with Lee in front, then Penny, then Jesse watching behind them. Lee opened the door, and the three stepped through the black space to the door to the next car. The door, which opened inward, creaked as Lee pushed it open.

The car was dark, but in a flash of light, there, in front of them, stood the conductor, with his dead black eyes and horrifying smile on his face.

"Hi, kids! I'm sorry to say you are not allowed in this car. This is our spacious first-class car, and your tickets are not first class. So back you go to your car!"

Horrified, the trio ran back to where they had been sitting together.

The conductor came to their row, leaned over, and whispered, "Nice try."

Penny buried her head in her hands and began to sob.

"I'm never going to get off this train. I'm never going to see my family again. I should have listened to the old legend and never come to see this train."

Lee put his arm around her.

"Shhh, now, it'll be okay. We're not done trying yet. There's gotta be more than one way to skin this cat."

Penny dried her eyes.

"Well, I guess we've got plenty of time to figure something out, huh."

Jesse, who was still facing the back of the train car, leaned over toward the aisle and furrowed his brow. Lee saw him.

"What's wrong, Jesse?"

"What's that room right there?" Jesse asked, pointing toward a small space behind the last seat. It had a narrow door with a small wooden handle.

Penny turned to look.

"It's apparently a bathroom. I'm guessing it's like an outside john, just a wooden seat with a hole in it. I've never had the courage to open the door to look."

Jesse turned around to make sure the conductor wasn't in sight, then got up and walked to bathroom, opened the door, and peeked in. As soon as the door opened, the sound of the train got louder.

Jesse looked around the little room then looked up. Lee and Penny watched as he turned his head a couple of times as he looked up. Then he came back out, closed the door, and slipped back over to his seat.

"Okay," Jesse said excitedly, "Penny, I don't blame you for not looking before. It's nothing pleasant. But you'll be interested to know there appears to be an access panel in the ceiling. I'm guessing you heard how loud it was in that room, yes?"

Lee and Penny nodded.

"I think the panel leads to the roof of the car. Like directly outside. If the panel will open, and we stand on the seat, I think we can lift ourselves onto the roof of the train. We could jump from there!"

"This train is going so fast," Lee said, "and there are trees all around. We might get hurt or killed jumping off."

"We'll die for sure if we stay here, Lee," Penny said. "I've been here long enough, and I'm willing to take the chance."

"Alright, then." Lee nodded. "Let's do it. But I think we gotta be careful about this. We can't all stand there waiting to climb up."

"What are you thinking, then?" Jesse asked.

"I'd say one of us goes in there first to see if the panel can be removed. If so, and if it leads to the roof, then gently knock on the door twice. Then climb up onto the roof. The next person waiting counts to ten, then gets up and enters the room, knocks twice, then climbs out. And so on till all three of us are on the roof. Then we jump together."

"Sounds like an excellent idea." Jesse grinned. "Lee, you go first. Penny, you follow. I brought up the rear when we tried to go to the back car, so I'll bring up the rear again and watch out for our spooky friend."

"Are you sure, Jesse?" Penny looked concerned.

"You bet. It'll be fine."

"Okay, let's hope this works," Jesse said quietly as he stood up. Looking around, he stepped over to the bathroom and went in, closing the door behind him.

The room was exactly as Penny had described. Small and cramped, only one person would fit. Against the wall was a bench with a hole in it, which opened to the outside below. It was just like an old outside toilet. Looking up, Lee saw the access panel Jesse told them about. It appeared to be just wide enough for Lee's shoulders to fit through, so it was definitely a manhole designed for someone to crawl through.

Lee stood up on the bench, being careful to avoid the hole, and put his hands up against the panel to see if it would move. He pushed up, trying to pop it out, but it wouldn't budge. Then he tried sliding it, to see if it slid to one side or the other. Sliding to the right, it budged slightly. Then it moved more. Finally, Lee was able to slide the panel completely out of the way. He was greeted by a rush of air as he could see the foggy night flying by above the speeding train.

Lee stepped off the bench, tapped on the bathroom door twice, then pulled himself up through the hole to the roof. The roof of the car was flat, and despite the rushing of the train, Lee was able to steady himself without any problem.

Within ten seconds, Penny appeared below in the bathroom. She rapped on the door then held her arms up so Lee could help her get up onto the roof. Once Penny was settled on the roof, both of them leaned down to help Jesse when he appeared.

After ten seconds, there was no Jesse.

When Penny got up and went into the bathroom, Jesse started counting to ten after hearing the two soft raps on the door. Then he looked around the train car.

"There are still six souls sitting in here," Jesse muttered to himself. "What are they going to do if we escape? Are they just going to die here?"

He walked over and sat down next to the bald old man.

"Hey, mister," Jesse said, nudging the man, "We're trying to escape. Do you want to come."

The old man lifted his head and looked at Jesse. His eyes were sad, but he smiled gently.

"Son," he said softly, "I'm an old man. M'wife died years ago. I've got no kids, no kin. I loved this train when I was your age. I'm okay to stay here. Good luck though."

The old man put his head back down as Jesse patted him on the shoulder.

Looking around, he moved over to the younger man across the aisle. He appeared to be in his 30s and was dressed well.

Jesse nudged him as well and tried to get his attention. The man looked startled.

"You're really trying to get out of here?" he asked, brushing his hair aside.

"Yes! You wanna come?"

"Oh, hell yes! I've got a wife and kids!"

Jesse walked the man back to the door of the bathroom and told him what to do.

Lee and Penny were still looking down into the bathroom, whispering "Jesse!" when the younger man's face appeared. Lee and Penny looked at each other then understood what Jesse was doing.

They helped the man up onto the roof and told him to crawl to the side so more people could fit up there. Then they looked down into the hole again to see who was coming along to escape.

Out of the six people who Jesse saw still sitting in the car, four wanted to try to escape with them, so one by one, each was pulled up and moved away from the hole.

Finally, Jesse's face appeared in the hole, and Lee reached down to help him onto the roof. He was about halfway up when the bathroom door flew open and the conductor jumped in and grabbed Jesse's legs, pulling him back in.

"Shit, he's got me!" Jesse screamed as he held on to Lee.

"Kick him! Kick the son of a bitch!" Lee yelled as he held on, trying to pull Jesse up.

Jesse squirmed and kicked as hard as he could, but the conductor held on, grinning the whole time.

"I can't – I'm losing my grip!" Jesse screamed as he tried to get away from the ghoul.

"Don't you give up, Jesse Trowbridge! I got you through second grade, I'm not letting go of you now!" Lee held on for dear life.

Jesse kept kicking, then the conductor's grip slipped on Jesse's leg, just enough to give him the chance to land a foot square in the conductor's face, sending him backward into the aisle.

"Pull!" Jesse yelled.

Penny joined in and grabbed an arm as both of them

pulled him up.

Once on the roof, the three of them stood up.

"There's not much time! That bastard is going to be up here in a matter of seconds! Are all you people ready to jump?"

The four people Jesse rescued stood up and nodded at Lee.

"Then let's *gooooooooooo*!" Lee yelled.

All seven of them jumped just as the conductor's ghoulish head poked up out of the access panel.

Expecting to hit trees, rocks, and whatever else, everyone landed on the ground with a thud and rolled a little. One by one, they got up on their knees and looked around. Surprised by the soft landing, they were even more surprised to discover they were not in the woods at all. They had landed in a grassy meadow and saw the lights of a town on the hill to their north. Walking toward it, Lee became aware he recognized some of the buildings.

"Jesse, Penny, that's Chadwick," Lee said, pointing.

"How the hell is that possible?" Jesse asked. "We passed Chadwick hours ago at breakneck speed on the train."

"Couldn't tell you," Lee said. "Maybe we weren't traveling so fast after all. Maybe it was an illusion. Or maybe we were there so long, it circled back again. Makes me wonder how much time has passed."

"Well, boys, I don't care how much time has passed. See that road right there?" Penny asked, pointing. "That's my road. I'm going to go home to my parents."

Penny stepped over to the boys and gave each one a hug, saving Lee for the last.

"Thanks for saving me," she whispered in his ear.

"You take care of yourself, Penny."

She pulled away and smiled.

"Maybe I'll see you again sometime soon," she said

with a wink.

"I sure hope so." Lee grinned and watched her as she turned and started down the road to her house, at first at a walk, then at a run.

The four people who jumped with them walked off into the night as the boys took the old Black Bear Trail to Sparta. It was daylight when they crept through Lee's bedroom window. Changing into clean clothes, they stepped out of Lee's room and walked into the kitchen. Lee's mom was making breakfast as his dad sat at the table, drinking coffee and reading the newspaper and didn't look up when Lee and Jesse walked in the room and sat down.

Lee quickly glanced at the calendar on the wall. His mother scribbled the weather every evening. She had written something for July 17th but hadn't yet for the 18th. It was just the next morning. They had only been gone a few hours.

They knew they were lucky to have escaped so quickly.

Lee's mom stepped out of the room for a moment. His dad set his paper down and looked at the boys.

"Interesting fog last night, huh, boys."

"Yes, sir," Lee answered.

Lee looked at his dad then Jesse, as Jesse looked at Lee then his dad.

After a few seconds of awkward silence, Lee's dad went back to his paper. Then he spoke up again.

"From the looks on your faces, I'm guessing you're not going to be too anxious to listen for that whistle again…"

He set his paper down again and looked at the boys.

"Are you?"

"No, sir," both boys answered.

Lee's dad grinned. As his smile got larger, Lee could see the rotted, gray teeth inside his black mouth. His dad suddenly leaped across the table, got in Lee's face, and yelled, "You're never getting off this train!"

Lee jolted awake. The conductor was leaning over in front of him.

"Enjoy the ride!" he laughed as he straightened up and walked to the front of the car.

Lee looked around the dimly lit car. All the people were still sitting upright, with their heads down, including Jesse, as the train sped along into the foggy night.

PHOBIA

— • ● • —

"I'm afraid of heights. Are you afraid of anything?"

Eli turned and looked at the man next to him at the bar. Sitting there in silence for several minutes, he was surprised by the sudden bizarre question from the stranger.

The man turned and looked at him.

"So are you afraid of anything?"

"Not really," Eli answered blandly.

"Nothing? You're not afraid of anything?"

"Well, maybe this qualifies: I'm terribly claustrophobic. I hate tight spaces."

"Yeah." The man nodded. "That's a good one."

The two men fell silent again.

Eli called the bartender over.

"I'm heading for the bathroom. If no one else takes my seat while I'm gone, set me up with another bourbon. Neat."

When he returned from the bathroom, his seat was still open, and a glass of bourbon awaited him.

As he settled in and picked up the glass to drink, the man next to him spoke up again.

"Cheers!" He raised his glass as Eli took a sip. "Here's to claustrophobia."

Eli gave him a puzzled look as a slight grin crept across the man's face.

Within seconds, Eli's eyelids felt heavy.

"Oh shit," he whispered as everything went black.

Eli's eyes wouldn't open. His mind felt sluggish, as if he had been asleep for days. Every breath felt like a chore, and his heart thumped hard but slowly.

As the seconds ticked by, he became aware of two things: he couldn't see, and he couldn't move. He wanted to move. His fingers and toes could move, but his ankles and wrists were confined, taped or strapped. His nose itched and he wanted to scratch it.

Taking stock of his situation, he could tell he was sitting in a chair and was strapped to it. He couldn't move his legs or his upper torso.

Worst of all, his head was taped up completely, except for his nostrils and his ears. Everything else was taped over. His eyes and his mouth were completely taped shut, and his head was strapped or taped to the chair.

Dammit. That guy put something in my drink. Thanks for asking me what I was afraid of, asshole.

Eli tried to remain calm.

Okay, so now what? This guy most likely stole my money and my identification while I was out. What else does he want with me? Does he want me to be scared? I'm restrained but I can't tell if I'm in a small space or a warehouse. Stay calm, Eli. It's a warehouse. You got this.

A nearby door opened then closed. He heard quiet footsteps approaching.

I was right. It's a big room.

The footsteps approached and walked around him a couple of times.

He is watching me, to see if I'm scared. Might wonder if I'm breathing hard. Guess what, asshole! I'm not! Failed this one!

The footsteps stopped. Eli strained to listen. He knew the person was still there. He heard faint noises, something moving. Then he felt a quick pain, like a pinprick. Then sleepiness again.

Eli blinked a couple of times as he regained consciousness. His eyes couldn't focus. His mind again felt sluggish, as if he had been asleep for days. The tape around his head was gone. He could breathe, albeit laboriously, through his mouth and could almost hear his heart thumping.

A few more blinks, and he felt like he could keep his eyes open. But once again, his body could not move. His arms and his legs were completely pinned down. He tried to move his hands and feet, but he could not. Only his head moved.

The sheet. The sheet covering him – he guessed it was a sheet – was so tight over him, he could barely breathe. Tiny drops of sweat began to break out on his forehead.

The room was completely dark. Had he been able to move, he could not have seen his hand in front of his face.

Why the hell is this thing so tight? It doesn't feel like cloth. Congratulations. I'm once again confined.

A door opened then latched closed. He heard footsteps.

"Hey!" Eli called out, his voice raspy.

The footsteps stopped. Whoever was in the blackened room, they heard him.

"Hey, can you please help me here? I - I can't move. This is really uncomfortable."

The footsteps moved again, closer to him, then a few steps away.

Another door opened then closed. It didn't sound like the first one.

He didn't hear any more footsteps.

LIGHT

Suddenly there was bright white light everywhere. Eli squeezed shut his stinging eyes as they began to water. He blinked a few times, wishing he could move his arms so he could wipe his eyes. A couple more blinks, and he was able to slowly open his eyes, squinting at first, then opening all the way, to discover his surroundings.

What the hell?

He was in a tight circular enclosure. Like a small lighted tunnel of some sort. He could tell he was lying on a hard surface, and the material covering him was a white rubbery sheet, stretched tight over him. His arms were pressed up against his sides, and the only thing he could move, aside from his head, was his fingers. He could wiggle them just a little.

Then the thing, the tube he was in, began to roar as he noticed little bars of light rotate over him. To his horror, he realized his situation.

My God, I'm strapped down in some kind of machine, like an MRI.

Eli was not a stranger to an MRI. He had been scanned before, after an injury while playing football. But he hadn't been restrained like this, nor had he awakened inside the machine with no explanation.

Who the hell is this guy? Why am I here? What has happened to me?

"Hey! Hey, I know you can hear me! Why am I here? What has happened to me?"

His heart pounded and he dripped with sweat. He could not hear anything over the roar of the machine as the little bars of light rotated faster over him.

The area of the tube directly over his face lit up bright white then faded to reveal a monitor. It only took a moment for Eli to realize he was being shown the scan of his body in real time. He could see everything from head to toe.

Then he saw it. In the area of his abdomen. A black mass. It had no discernable shape. He couldn't really make out what organs it was near. But it was clearly a mass. And it was moving. He couldn't feel it, but it was moving inside him.

Holy shit!

"Hey! Get me out of here! What the hell is this thing moving around in me? Hey, can you hear me?"

The screen went dark, and the machine began to wind down, finally ending its rotation. The table upon which he lay began to slide out of the machine, and Eli felt cool air on his sweat-drenched face for the first time since he awakened. He longed to move his arms and wipe the sweat from his face and hoped whoever was in the control room would soon come out and free him from the sheet restricting him so intensely.

But no.

Just as he began to calm down, the table began to slowly slide back into the machine. Eli closed his eyes and tried to keep from hyperventilating as he slipped deeper and deeper into the narrow tube.

Relax, Eli, relax.

He tried to calm himself down, but at this point, all he could think about was getting out of the tube and out from under the sheet.

The tube began to rotate over him, and the screen lit up again. This time, it showed just his abdomen area and the moving mass. Eli looked closely. The mass churned and moved, almost like a heavy viscous fluid. Then he saw it. An arm.

He couldn't hold back a scream.

"What the hell is this? Somebody answer me!"

The machine wound down again as the screen went black. The table began to move him out again, slower than the first time.

These people are clearly screwing with me.

Taking what felt like an agonizing sixty seconds, the table finally cleared the machine, and Eli was out in the fresh air. He lay still, drenched with sweat, looking around to see if anyone was coming to set him free.

The lights went out again, plunging the room into complete darkness. He heard a door open and close and footsteps approaching from behind him.

Must be whoever was in the control room. Better not say anything too hateful. They might stick me back in that goddamn thing.

He lay quietly, waiting for whatever happened next.

Suddenly he felt a sharp pain in his neck, as if he had been stuck with something again.

Then everything went black.

Eli began to awaken, again lying down. This time, it felt softer, and in his clouded mind, he detected no restraint. He opened his eyes and sat up quickly.

"Easy there, Eli, don't sit up too fast. Take your time."

The voice was male, deep, and soothing. Eli rubbed his eyes, happy to be able to move his arms. He ran his hands over his face, dropped his arms, and opened his eyes.

He was in an office. Fine oak bookcases lined the walls. A large oak desk sat to his left, and across the room, in a plush high-backed chair, sat a man.

Eli looked closely at him. He was the man from the bar who asked him what he was afraid of. Clearly the man knew his name, but otherwise, Eli had no idea who he was. With dark, swept-back hair, large plastic-rimmed glasses, the man sat upright in his chair looking at Eli with a slight grin.

"Who are you?" Eli asked.

"I'm Doctor William Sperry. Welcome to my research project."

"Research project? I never agreed to be part of any project! You slipped something into my drink at the bar and then kidnapped me!"

Doctor Sperry looked at Eli for a moment.

"On the contrary. Just before you passed out at the bar, I asked you if you'd like me to take you somewhere. You nodded. So, you see, you consented."

"You waited until I was under the influence of whatever you gave me…"

"Sodium pentothal."

" – Sodium whatever. I think your constituents would consider such activity quite illegal."

"That may be true if I had constituents. I work independently."

Eli stopped for a moment and scratched his head.

"What was that machine, and that thing inside me?"

"Thing inside you?" Dr. Sperry looked puzzled.

"When I was in that MRI thing. On the screen. It showed me a mass in my stomach."

Eli reached down and lifted his shirt, looking for an incision. There were no signs of anything. Just his skin.

"Perhaps the relaxant made you see things." Dr. Sperry scribbled a note on his phone.

"I don't know what you gave me, but clearly the screen showed me a mass. And it had an arm or leg or something. It was moving, though I didn't feel it."

"Don't worry, Eli. You're fine."

"Ok, if I'm fine, would you mind telling me why you did those things to me?"

"I'm studying reactions to phobias, how people act when they face their phobias, or when they think they are facing their phobias."

"So that's why you had me taped up but in a big room."

"You could tell you were in a big room?"

"Yeah. Your footsteps and the echo gave it away. I was confined, but I knew I wasn't in a small space. So it didn't bother me as much as the machine did."

"Interesting. I have to make a note of that." Sperry wrote more notes on his phone. Eli watched as the doctor mouthed the note he was typing.

This guy is completely nuts.

"Would you like something to drink, Eli?"

Doctor Sperry got up and walked to a cabinet, opening the door to reveal a refrigerator stocked with various soft drinks and bottles of water.

"At this point, I'd really like some water."

Sperry grabbed a bottle of water and set it down on the shelf above the refrigerator. He turned his back to Eli to remove the lid then turned around and brought the water to him.

"Enjoy. I'm sure you're thirsty."

Eli jumped up and tackled Sperry and pinned him to the floor.

"What were you planning to do, *Doctor*?" Eli snidely emphasized the word. "What did you put in my water when you turned your back to me?"

"I didn't put anything in your water." Sperry struggled to get up.

"Oh really? Then you won't mind drinking it yourself!"

Eli shoved the water bottle into Sperry's mouth, squeezing it to force the water in. He then threw the empty bottle across the room and covered Sperry's mouth to force him to swallow it.

Within seconds, Sperry's eyes got heavy, and he was soon unconscious.

The remains of a man with dark hair were found at the base of a tall transmission tower, discovered by the farmer whose land the structure stood upon. When the sheriff began investigating the grisly scene, he found the man to be void of any wallet or identification. Searching further, a piece of paper was found in the man's shirt. A simple message was scrawled on the sheet:

"So – you're afraid of heights?"

THE BRIDGE

•●•

Wha – How – How the hell did I get here? And while we're at it, where the hell is Here?

Ugh, my God my head hurts. It's – it's behind my right eye, this throbbing pain. It – it feels like somebody's pinching a raw nerve with tweezers. I swear every time my heart thumps, I get this lightning flash of pain behind my eye. *Thump. Flash. Thump. Flash. Thump. Flash.*

I – I don't know if I can stand up. My arms, my legs, they feel like rubber. It's as if I have no strength.

God, what is this place? Everything is wet, and the fog is so thick, I cannot see more than five feet in front of me... or behind me, or beside me... or below me.

I woke up to find myself completely drenched with sweat, in a daze, and on this rickety old bridge. The boards are nasty, slimy, like they've been coated by millions of slugs. These ropes – who knows how long they've been here. I'm amazed this damn thing holds me...

Ugh, I gotta try to stand up.

Come on, legs, work. I pull myself up with trembly arms to get upright. Holding on to the ropes for dear life, I'm up.

Thump. Flash. Thump. Flash. Thump. Flash.

Now what?

I look behind me. All I see is this crappy bridge and fog. I look in front of me. More crappy bridge and more fog. Dammit!

I struggle to breathe in the cold wet air. My legs tremble, knees wanting to buckle, as I fight the pain in my head.

And this godforsaken bridge keeps swaying every time I move.

I take a meek step forward, inching my toes along, squinting through the fog in hopes of catching a glimpse of something before me, some indication of where I am, where I've been… or how high I am above something…

The pain in my head, behind my eye, tortures me.

Thump. Flash. Thump. Flash. Thump. Flash.

Creeping forward, I hear screaming through the mist. It comes from everywhere, nowhere, above and below. Looking behind me does no good. There is only forward, or at least, I think so…

What if forward is actually backward, and what if I was supposed to go back that way instead of this way, and what if – ugh, my head.

Another step, and the boards, almost mossy under my bare feet, make unsettling squishing sounds, as if their saturation has weakened them beyond the capacity to support my weight. I don't want to fall. Please don't let me fall.

Thump. Flash. Thump. Flash. Thump. Flash.

I wish I could hear something. No, not the screams again. I want to hear something else, anything else. Running water, a breeze through tree limbs, the buzz of a mosquito just before it bites my ear. Anything. Ichabod Crane at least had the sound of his horse's hooves as he ventured into those dark, sinister woods. I want to hear something.

A chill runs up my spine as I become aware of someone's hot breath on the back of my neck. I turn quickly to face the specter, rocking the bridge wildly.

No one is there.

And it's getting darker.

Thump. Flash. Thump. Flash. Thump. Flash.

I turn back around and tighten my grip on the ropes.

Another scream blasts through the mist, swimming around me in the dank air, and I want to cover my ears.

But I don't dare let go of the ropes.

The smell of Death wafts into my nostrils, but I know not from where. Over what do I cross? What horrors surely await me below if only I could see them? Am I perilously traversing over some field where the dead lay in silence? Is it some carnage-filled lake teeming with destroyed wildlife, their spoiled bodies floating with glassed-over eyes seeing past me into nothingness? Or am I smelling what's left of those who tried to cross this bridge before me?

Thump. Flash. Thump. Flash. Thump. Flash.

The board below my right foot snaps under my weight. My left foot slips on its wet plank, and I almost lose my grip on the ropes. Dear God, don't let me fall!

Breathe. Just breathe.

Mustering up what's left of my strength, I pull on the ropes, swinging my dangling legs up, back onto the bridge, moving forward quickly, to get away from the spot. How many more boards will snap beneath me?

Thump. Flash. Thump. Flash. Thump. Flash.

It's getting darker. Still no sound, save for the wretched screams piercing the fog, live within the fog, surround me like the fog. I'll take the silence if the screaming will stop.

I continue to move forward, knowing not where I'm going, nor where I've been, nor why I'm here. The pain in my head clouds my thinking, and my entire world has collapsed into this small, slimy, fog-enshrouded place, and each step I take.

Thump. Flash. Thump. Flash. Thump. Flash.

Screams once again pierce the fog, like a clap of thunder from a nearby lightning strike. They don't stop but continue deliriously in wail after wail after goddamn wail, with barely a breath taken between. The screams become more hoarse, more desperate, more exhausted, more horrified.

My throat burns, I cough hard, doubling over, struggling to catch my breath.

I hear another scream and in the horror of that moment, I recognize its source – it's coming from within me. They've all been from me.

Thump. Flash.

I scream again, owning my anguish, letting it out with everything within me.

Thump. Flash.

I stand now silent, exhausted, panting.

Thump. Flash.

The light wanes.

Thump. Flash.

My grip on the ropes tightens.

Thump. Flash. Thump. Flash. Thump. Flash.

With the last glimmer of daylight, the fog suddenly clears, and I can see everything around me, above me, below me –

Oh shit –

THE SPEARS LAKE INCIDENT

—————— •●• ——————

My friend Myra loved going to the Spears Lake Wilderness Area to hike the trails, and I loved going with her. I only marginally like to hike. I very much like being with Myra. Unfortunately, she has no idea how I feel about her. She thinks I'm just a friend. Truthfully, I want to be more than a friend, but I cannot bring myself to say it. I know it would screw up the friendship, and I'm not willing to do that. So, I keep my feelings for her to myself – and we hike.

Several trails wound their way through the wilderness area, and led hikers to the lake itself, or to a large meadow with pretty wildflowers, or deep into the Ponderosa Pine forest, or along the Nibo Vai River, the tributary for Spears Lake. One thing Myra loved about the area was how the trails were laid out, as none of them crossed each other. The Lake Trail, which was three miles long, went only to the lake and back. The Nibo Vai Trail, a hardy five miles in length, went only to the river and back. Unlike other wilderness areas where trails crisscross one another, this location provided the hiker with a true feeling of oneness with nature. As I said, she loved it. Frankly, the isolation freaked me out a little.

Myra has always been a pro at packing for a hike. She typically has enough water for both of us, sunscreen, solar-powered battery backup for her phone, a first aid kit, binoculars, and bear spray. On the other hand, I feel like I'm lucky if I remember to wear the right walking shoes.

One Saturday last month, we took the Lake Trail,

expecting the area to be void of many hikers due to the chilly weather. Myra was her normal eager self. She maintained her typical ten to twelve paces ahead of me, occasionally looking back and asking, "Are you still back there, buddy?"

By mid-morning, we were only half a mile from the lake, where the left edge of the trail drops off into a small meadow. Since she's more of a woodsy girl, she spent her time looking to the right, into the trees. I decided to look toward the meadow and stopped when a large mass caught my eye. I have hiked this trail with Myra multiple times, and have looked at that meadow often, but never before saw a large mass on the ground.

"Hey, Myra!" I called out, because I knew she wouldn't look back to see where I was for a bit. I turned and saw her stop and look back at me. I waved her over, and she came bouncing my way.

"Do you see that big mass over there?" I asked, pointing.

"Yep, I see it."

"Good, that means I'm not crazy. Dig your binoculars out, will you?"

The smile on Myra's face was gone once she noticed how serious I was. Within a few seconds, she pulled out her binoculars, and I took a closer look.

It was big, really big, and brown and furry. And asleep.

"Myra, get out your bear spray."

I figured with my luck, we would make just enough noise to wake this thing up, and then it would be unhappy. Of course, it never occurred to me that yelling at Myra should have woken it up.

Just then, a hawk swooped down and landed on the thing. It didn't move.

"Oh shit, I think they've got a dead bear here."

Even though all hikers are supposed to stay on the trails, I couldn't help but want to see this thing up close, so we stepped off the trail and started walking toward the bear. The hawk looked at us, gave a high-pitched squawk, and took off.

As we got closer, we could tell the bear was lying with its back toward us and seemed curled up into a ball, almost like a fetal position. As we walked around it, I noticed how massive its feet were, nearly twice the size of my hand. Standing in front of it, we were greeted by an awful sight. Its body had been ripped open from its neck down to its lower belly. Worst of all, however, was the fact that its head was missing.

Against my better judgement, I reached out and touched the bear.

"This thing is still warm." I turned and looked at Myra. "He hasn't been dead for very long."

A feeling of dread came over me as I stood up and looked around. For a radius of about fifteen feet, everything was flattened. The grass, the wildflowers, all were flattened. A log lying a few feet behind the bear was shattered.

"Whatever happened, he put up a big damn fight. Look at all this, Myra."

"Who could have done such a thing?"

"I don't think it's a question of who, Myra. We didn't pass anyone going back the other way. I haven't heard any voices out here. I don't think anyone else is here. So instead of who did this, *what* did this. And what bothers me even more is whether or not it is still nearby."

I looked around for tracks leading away from the scene. Aside from our tracks from walking over to the bear, there was nothing visible to show where the killer, whatever it was, left the scene.

"Look, Evan, there's no blood here. There should be lots of blood. This was too violent for there to not be any blood."

"Yeah. Let's get out of here and report the bear to the

ranger."

"Wait, I hate to spoil a good walk because a dead bear was found. Let me just call." Myra dug out her phone and started to punch in the number for the ranger station at the parking lot then stopped.

"I don't have any signal."

I put my hand up.

"Myra, do you hear that?"

We both stood and listened.

"I don't hear anything."

"Exactly. No birds chirping. That noisy hawk is gone. Dead silence."

My heart thumped a little harder, and a single bead of sweat broke out on my forehead.

While standing by the decapitated bear, looking at the surrounding woods, something hit the back of my head.

"What the hell was that?" I spun around and looked into the woods then down at my feet.

"What happened?"

"Something just hit me in the back of the head!"

Both of us looked around on the ground.

"Could this be it?" Myra picked up a small stone and showed it to me.

"Whatever hit me wasn't very big," I said, rubbing the back of my head. "That's probably it."

"Who would throw a little thing like this at you, out here?"

She no more got those words out of her mouth when something hit her in the back of the head.

"Ouch!" She jumped and felt the back of her head.

I looked down and found another stone similar to the one she found.

"Same guy?" she asked.

"Don't know. These stones came from two different directions. And I'm telling you, this may not be a person at all. Come on, Myra, let's get out of here. But don't run.

This thing may decide we are next and chase us. Let's just walk away and let it have its prize bear here."

We started walking slowly back to the trail. After just a few steps, each of us was hit by another stone.

"Damn!" I said, rubbing the side of my head. "It was from over there to the right this time."

"No, it wasn't," Myra protested. "It hit me in the left side of my head."

"Shit, there may be more than one." I looked all around as we finally made it back to the trail and started the two-and-a-half-mile trek back to the parking lot and ranger station.

We didn't run; we definitely walked quicker than a casual hike, but we didn't run. I kept looking back over my shoulder to see if something was coming up behind us but didn't see anything. I heard a large branch snap to my right and looked quickly into the thick woods. Was something moving about fifty feet away? I couldn't tell for sure, but the sound of the branch snapping got my attention. I started breathing harder.

The trail ahead curved slightly to the left and as we looked, something darted across the path.

Myra stopped, tears running down her face.

"Evan, did you see that?"

"Yes."

"What was it?"

"I don't know. Not human."

"Evan – I – I think we're being hunted."

I turned Myra toward me and cradled her tear-stained cheeks in my hands.

"Myra, I'm not going to let anything happen to you. We've only got less than two miles to go. We can do this. Let's go."

Myra sniffed and nodded then took my hand, and we started walking, more quickly now, toward the trailhead.

We started hearing more branches snap on either side

of us, and I could swear I heard little low chuffs as well. Whatever was in the woods, it was staying out of sight but somehow was in the clear long enough to keep throwing rocks at us. We got hit on the sides of our faces, our shoulders, and arms, and I took one hit in the hip.

Then the rocks started getting bigger.

I noticed the larger rocks when one hit me square in the middle of my back. I didn't stop to look, but I knew whatever threw it had to have been standing in the middle of the trail behind us.

"Shit, Myra, the rocks are getting bigger!"

"Oh God, Evan! We're never going to make it. They are going to kill us!"

"We've got about a mile to go. Come on, Myra, let's *run!*"

We broke into a full sprint, still holding hands, as the rocks kept flying around us. We were about three hundred yards from the parking lot and ranger station when a big rock came flying through and hit Myra in the head, knocking her down. Blood immediately began to pour from the wound, so I knelt down and pulled my handkerchief out of my back pocket and held it up to her head. She was dazed but conscious. I became aware of several high-pitched howls coming from the woods all around me.

"Myra, honey, I need you to hold this on your head. You're bleeding quite a bit."

"Just leave me, Evan. Leave me so they can have me. You get away."

"Oh hell no!"

I grabbed her and with a big grunt, I hoisted her up over my shoulder and started running again.

I've heard stories about how at moments of extreme duress, a person can perform nearly superhuman acts. I think that's what happened, because I'm not a great runner, and Myra is not light. But nonetheless, I somehow managed to run full speed the last three hundred yards to the parking lot. There were no cars except for mine, and the ranger station was closed. I laid Myra down in the back seat.

"Myra, honey, the ranger station is closed. I'm going to drive you to Ingalls. It's only twenty miles and they have a hospital there."

She moaned, holding the handkerchief to her head as I closed the door.

Walking around the car, I stopped and looked toward the woods, at the trailhead. That's when I saw them.

Some were standing; others were crouching. Five of them, with big rocks in their hands or paws or whatever they were. They saw what I did; they saw me pick her up and run full speed with her. Now, they were in the open, looking at me.

The one in the middle took a step forward, dropped its rock, then looked at me, and I swear it nodded.

I nodded back then got in the car and sped off to Ingalls. After I knew Myra was stable and cared for, I called the Forestry office.

Spears Lake Wilderness Area is now permanently closed, and the locals still tell stories in low tones about rangers that went in to investigate but never returned.

To Find a Song

Is there a song to sing,
At this beautiful moment?
Is there some melody,
A dirge perhaps,
Within the bowels of uncertainty?

May the pendulum swing,
To and fro,
Fro and to,
As the time counts down
That which is left.

Is there a song to sing,
Or is it but folly
Of my mind?
Rusty,
Old,
Unused,
The pipes grow silent.

I know not the pitch,
I feel not the rhythm,
Yet the song wells up
Within my soul,
Within the well
Of my soul.

My lungs expand;
My old lungs,
Coughing,
Half-filled
With sputum
Of a million breaths
And their toxins carried into
The vacuum.

A cough;
A moment as I turn,
Expectorating;
Another cough,
Harder than the last;
And another breath
Deeper
In search of song.

Starts low, it does,
The song deep within.
Close my eyes, I must.
Open my arms, I must.
Laugh within my mind, I must,
To imagine the sight
Of my attempt at music.

The sound,
My song,
From deep within,
Grows stronger.

In a moment,
It reaches full strength,
Full volume,
And the pitch,
That pitch previously known not even to myself,

Is found
And projected
At great volume.
And even with eyes closed,
I sense that all that surrounds me
Is illuminated
In this singular moment
Of glorious song.

My glorious song,
My final song,
I scream
As I stand on the tracks
Facing the fast-approaching train.

THE DINNER

• ● •

A Tale in Four Acts

Act One: The Remote Observer

I couldn't help but notice them when we sat down.

My wife and I were in Leadville, Colorado, for a nice getaway. One night, we stopped at a trendy restaurant on the main drag in the historic district, and despite not having reservations, were seated quickly. Amongst tables and booths, we settled into a high-top, which gave me ample view of the surroundings.

That's when I noticed the couple sitting in a booth behind my wife.

The first thing to catch my attention was they weren't looking at each other and not saying a word; they were too absorbed in their phones to notice one another.

Mind you, I'm not trying to knock anyone for being on their phones. I know it happens. My wife is on her phone a lot, handling her business. That's just the way it is.

But this was different. I felt a big wall between these two. It hurt to watch them.

Soup showed up. They lowered their heads and began to eat.

Still silence between them.

No, I didn't stare. My wife and I visited as we normally do then ordered our food and agreed our waiter had a great personality.

But every few seconds, I had to glance to see what was

119

happening at the booth, hoping to see something resembling affection... or at least acknowledgement of each other.

The wife spoke a couple of times. The husband nodded without looking up, so I began to study him a bit more...

He was a good-sized guy. He appeared to be average height – hard to know when he's sitting – and just a tad overweight, like me. There was something about him and his demeanor. You know the type. The kind of guy who never smiles in photos, no matter how many around him are smiling. Not just quiet but too quiet. Closed off.

She appeared to be much shorter than him. She had soft features and looked kind, but tired.

The main course came for them and eliminated another opportunity to visit. They ate in silence, neither one finishing their food. Then they ordered dessert.

The restaurant played great music for atmosphere. It wasn't overly loud, but clear enough that each song was recognizable. After playing David Bowie and Queen singing "Under Pressure" – *how appropriate* – I recognized a reggae beat, and Bob Marley began to sing "Everything's Gonna Be Alright."

Their dessert arrived. The music continued to play.

When the chorus came around, I saw it. A spark. From her, not him. They were actually looking at each other for a moment, and she leaned forward with her head cocked and a twinkle in her eye. She mouthed the words with the song, "Everything's gonna be alright."

He looked back down and continued eating.

She looked back down and eventually started eating again.

He ate half of his dessert and pushed it aside. They both said something, then he began to talk more. He brought his arms up, resting his elbows on the table. As he spoke, his right hand reached over to his left hand and began to play with his wedding band. He twirled it around a couple of times, then pulled it forward, nearly off his finger, then pushed it back, and twirled it again.

The ring... moving the ring... in her face...

The conversation lasted only a few moments. If this was a marriage in crisis, she was awfully strong through the meal. Maybe this was just their normal way, and she was used to it.

Forced herself to accept it –

At about the time our dessert arrived, the couple's evening drew to a close. They both got up, grabbed their to-go boxes, and headed for the door, him in front. Once they were outside, she moved up beside him. Well, kind of beside him. One of his hands held his food, while the other stayed in his pocket, and there was at least a foot and a half between them.

Air is a good insulator...

Act Two: Her

Another dinner out together, and here we are, looking at our phones.

Something is bothering him, I know it. I just don't know what to do about it.

What is he thinking? What is he looking at on his phone? Is there someone else? Is he talking to her now? I've always trusted him, always loved him, and trusted he loves me. But now I'm worried. Whatever is wrong, we'll get through it.

Thank goodness the soup showed up. At least I can get him to tell me how he likes it.

Apparently not. He just won't talk. Please, my love, tell me what's wrong.

I can't stand this anymore.

"How's your soup?"

He says it's good, and that's it. I guess I might have better luck when the food shows up.

Ah, the food arrives!

My stomach is in such knots, I know I'm not going to be able to eat all of this.

"How's your steak, love?"

He said it's good, but he's just picking at it. He must be in knots too.

Please, please tell me.

Well, isn't that interesting! He wanted to order dessert! He never does that. Maybe he's going to tell me what's going on.

Act Three: Him

Oh my God. How am I going to tell her? What am I going to say? Honey, your husband is a failure? I'm supposed to be The Man. I'm supposed to provide. That's what I was always told. I saw it in my grandparents and my parents. It's my job to provide and protect, and if I can't do that, I'm not worth anything.

I'm going to have to tell her, but not yet. I can't. We need to get through this dinner.

She likes to look at her phone, so maybe while we wait, I'll do another job search. Surely something is out there, even if it's something different. I don't have to work in an office. I can do construction work. I can run equipment. I can do anything – except what I've been doing, apparently.

God, I'm in knots. Yes, the soup is good, but I can't even taste it. I don't know if I'll be able to taste anything. This is killing me. I wonder how much life insurance I have...

Why the hell did I order steak? This thing is huge. I doubt I can finish it.

Ok, I'm going to tell her. Not over this steak though.

"Dessert? Yes, let's have some. I'll have the cheesecake."

I'll tell her over dessert.

Act Four: Him and Her

Him, after thanking the waiter for dessert and beginning to eat: Honey, I have something I need to tell you. I – I lost my job today.

Her: Baby, is that what's been bothering you?

He nods.

Her: I knew something was wrong. You had me scared. But we will get through this. Don't be so upset. Do you want to tell me what happened?

Him: Well, there's not much to tell. Business is down, and they said something recently about possible downsizing. I wasn't too worried about it, especially after working for them for so long. But apparently their numbers show my accounts are down, down enough to be a good candidate for the downsizing. At the end of the day today, Mark had me come to his office, and Emily from HR was there, and they laid it all out for me. I got three month's severance, and an option to be on Cobra for insurance. And that was it. They made me put in a full day, knowing this was what they were planning to do.

Her: I'm so sorry, love.

Him: Now, I don't know what we're going to do.

Her, hearing the music playing, sings with the song, smiling: Everything's gonna be alright.

He sighs as they go back to eating their dessert.

Him, after finishing dessert, twirling his ring: I've been so upset about this because, you know, I was raised to believe I'm supposed to provide for us.

Her: Yes, love, but this is also the twenty-first century, and that's the old way of living. We still have my income while you look for something.

Him: You're not mad at me?

Her: Of course not!

Him: You're not ashamed of me?

Her: No! Never! I love you, and we are going to get through this.

He sighs and smiles.

Him: I've already done some looking on job searches but it's not showing much.

Her: Why don't you just rest for a couple of days? Decompress. You need to clear your head before you start looking. Okay?

Him, smiling: Okay. Your love never ceases to amaze me. Thank you.

Her: I love you.

Him: I love you too. Let's go home.

As they walk to the car, his hand is in his pocket, getting his keys out. Once settled in the car, they hold hands and don't let go till they get home.

What one sees from afar may never match reality...

BLESSING THE WRETCHES

———————— •●• ————————

Reverend Edward McKinley's soul felt tired after a long and very emotional day visiting people within the Brower County Jail. He had one visit left, so he straightened himself up as much as possible and put on a smile, as a middle-aged man walked in and sat down opposite him.

"How are you doing, Murray?" Ed asked, smiling.

"I'm hanging in there, Reverend," Murray answered. "How are you?"

The pastor let out a sigh.

"Oh, I must admit to you, Murray, I am a bit tired. I've been here all day visiting with folks. It's the duty which God has imposed upon me. It's very troubling, you know, to see these poor lost wretches, to feel their pain. I try very hard to give them hope, though I don't know if I'm succeeding much.

"It's so upsetting to see people under these circumstances. At times I worry somehow just being in this building somehow tarnishes my position with The Almighty. But I have to believe though I walk through the valley of the shadow of some awful people, no offense intended, I shall fear no evil.

"Murray, my own mother – I had a visit with my mother. My own flesh and blood mother, the woman who brought me into the world! Do you have any idea what kind of stain that is? To visit your mother within this jail? Do you realize how many prayers I have to send up just to make sure I'm not viewed as some sort of scourge for this?"

"How did your mother seem to be?" Murray asked.

"She cried a lot. Just sat there and cried. I tried to convince her that her sins were forgiven. That God forgave her, and even more importantly, I forgave her. She would nod a few times, maybe say my name here and there. That was it. Poor wretch."

"Who else have you talked with, Reverend?"

"Oh, let's see. There was Jimmy Robbins. Now let me tell you, he's got problems. With his wife and kids at home, I don't know how he shows his face, even in here. Then there was William – William – oh, what is his name? Talbot; that's it, Talbot! Did you know he's an elder in the church? An elder in my congregation, and I have to talk with him in here, for pity's sake."

Reverend McKinley leaned back in his chair for a moment.

"Oh, Murray, what am I going to do? Thank God I don't have to report these numbers to my superiors. I'd be out of a job in no time." He tried to chuckle. "I just don't get it. You know, I've been preaching for over 25 years now, and all of my messages have been divinely inspired. Yes, divinely inspired! God speaks and I hear Him! So, my messages, my divine messages, should be on the radio, or television! Imagine how many souls I could save if I was just on television! That's where I belong, not in my piddly little congregation, filled with ordinary people pestering me about their petty needs – again, no offense intended."

He broke into a false high voice.

"My husband is sick! I can't pay my bills! My wife is dying! My son is in trouble again! Blah blah blah, it goes on and on, Murray."

Murray sat back and folded his arms.

"This wasn't my lot in life, Murray. This isn't why I went to seminary. I went to be rich and famous and respected and paid well and to have a big staff playing interference so I wouldn't have to go through this crap of visiting people in a prison, no offense again. I'm just – I'm just too special for this, you know?"

Murray stayed quiet and nodded.

"You know who else I talked with today, Betsy Reynolds. Betsy Reynolds sat down in that very chair you are now sitting in. Wife, mother. Who knew I would see her in here. It was a surprise, I tell you. I didn't expect to see someone like her walking in here. I had no idea she had fallen off the good side of life. Yet here she sat."

"Did she have much to say?" Murray asked quickly.

"No, she didn't. I guess I did a lot of the talking. I wanted her to confess her sins, put it all on the table, let it out, you know. It's good for the soul! The Truth shall set you free, Murray. It says so somewhere in there in the Good Book. But as you might expect, she didn't want to say much, not in here where the guards could be listening. It's just as well, I suppose. She's probably afraid of me turning my back on her. It matters to folks, you know. They don't want someone like me passing judgement on them, scorning them, pointing out their failings. No, they don't want to hear that kind of thing. They want all the lovey-dovey stuff, sins forgiven, and on and on. But some people have to be told when they've done wrong, and I'm the man to do it."

"You know, with all due respect, Reverend, I haven't heard a lot of ministers talk about condemning. Most of them talk about forgiveness."

"I know, Murray, but somebody's got to take a stand. Somebody who's perfect and does nothing wrong, somebody like me; I've got to stand up and say to these people they are a disappointment to God, and I as a perfect specimen of faith have the right to throw the book at them, so to speak. It's not popular, but somebody's got to do it. These other preachers, claiming to have love in their hearts, let them take care of the poor and homeless and the countless others who want help. I lower myself enough making these visits, again no offense. But this isn't what I want. I'm destined for better."

"Sorry to hear you are so burdened, Reverend."

McKinley looked at Murray and smiled.

"I'm sorry, Murray, I didn't mean to rattle on so and sound like I wasn't pleased to see you. I guess I just had to get it out."

"I hope getting it out made you feel better, Reverend."

"It did, Murray. It sure did. So, tell me, how are you faring?"

"I'm doing ok." Murray nodded. "Nothing I need to burden you with."

"Well, that's good," McKinley said, nodding his head. "Tell me again, what are you in here for?"

"To see you, Reverend."

"Oh, I know, but I mean, what have they got you in jail for, Murray?"

"Hmm?" Murray frowned.

"Come on, Murray, you can tell me. What did you do to end up here in the pokey?"

"Uh, Reverend –" Murray stammered. "I'm not the one in jail. You are."

McKinley furrowed his brow.

"Did you think those people were in jail and you were visiting them?" Murray asked.

"Um. Uh, well yes. They're all in here, just like you, for doing something wrong."

Murray shook his head.

"Reverend, you're the one in jail. You don't remember what you did, do you?"

"I haven't done anything. I'm a perfect specimen of faith, with a direct line to God. I do nothing wrong."

"You killed your wife, Padre. You killed her and then

you nailed her to a cross in your front yard. Then the cops came, and they checked you out and figured out you were absolutely nuts. Once you're convicted, you're going to spend a long time at a special place."

Murray stood up and motioned to the guard.

"McKinley," Murray said, "All those people, those good people, your mom, Jimmy Robbins, William Talbot, Betsy Reynolds, and me, we all came by to see how you were doing. You're going back to your cell now, and I'm going to walk out of here."

As the guard turned McKinley to go, Murray stopped.

"And, Padre, all those other lower-level preachers you talked about – they don't kill their wives. And they love people, instead of lording over them. You'd better read the Good Book again and look for the parts about humility."

Murray shook his head as he heard McKinley yelling, "No!" repeatedly as the guard took him to his cell.

ON THE
LIGHTER
SIDE

The Fright

———— ◆◆◆ ————

Sitting at home one frightful night,
As I prayed for morning with all my might,
I at once spotted a horrible sight
As the lightning filled the sky.

The frightful sight that I did sighted
When the sky got bright as the lightning did lighted
Made me run to my room and under the bed I did hided
As the thunder roared.

Lying there shaking I started desirin'
That a great big lawman I could be hirin'
Then suddenly there came a loud siren
Passing by my abode.

The siren did not even stop the shape
That continued approaching in its black cape
And I knew at once I'd have to scratch and to scrape
To ever try to get away.

Then at once I knew that I oughter
Face this thing, this creeping marauder
And then the thing spoke and said, "Where's my
daughter?"

I knew 'twas deep shit now.

For this thing that I heard and this thing that I saw
That made me so cowardly under my bed crawl
Was the beast known as my mother-in-law
And I screamed with all that I had.

I hastily darted to the front door
To make my escape, but I hit the hard floor
After tripping over the large feet of her sister, Lenore,
Who promptly said, "Get up, dearie."

I shuddered and shook in this frightful night
As the Old Bat decided to turn on a light
And said, "We've come over to spend the night,"
And just then the thunder roared.

I knew that right then, my life, it was over,
And I longed for the times growing up in Dover,
Which is strange considering I grew up in Plover,
But that didn't matter right now.

I had to get out right then and right there,
For I knew this horror I could no longer bear,
But then my wife was standing at the top of the stairs,
And the thunder roared.

"Settle down, you little puff of a man,"
My wifey said with the taser in her hand.
"He'll be no more trouble to you, ma'am."
My wife gave her mother a grin.

My betrothed hit the button, the electrodes went zoom,
And I suddenly noticed a certain spin to the room
Then landed in front of Lenore's big shoes
And said, "Oh, size 14."

My beloved popped the taser once again
And watched as my testicles began to spin
Then her mom said with an evil grin,
"I guess that's enough."

They sent me to the basement without any food
Which put me in a really foul mood,
Especially when I heard the noisy brood
Break out the KFC.

The story is sad but oh, so true,
And beware, gentlemen, I'm talking to you,
As your fate might end up this way, too,

Beware when the thunder roars.

OH, THE FEAR, THE HORROR

—————————— •●• ——————————

My friend, hear me, and hear me well. This type of subject does not come up often, and it is well that it should not. For to make an admission of this nature to you is but a walk along a slippery slope. I speak in danger of losing your confidence, or worse, your respect. Yet I must offer up this confession, this bearing of the soul, this stripping away of all walls which protect my inner being. I do this in hope that you, my dear friend and brother, may learn from my example.

Tonight, as we sit here in this dimly lit social club, amongst our friends and peers, as well as those to whom we are anonymous, I make my admission. I admit to you a weakness; a weakness which is not necessarily uncommon. But alas, I fear I am perhaps the only one who is brave enough to admit it.

I admit to you I have a phobia. I have an uncontrollable fear rendering me powerless. It bids me physical trembling while I am awake, and worse yet, it fills me with night terrors as I attempt to lay in arms of Slumber.

I have a fear, a dread, a fright that paralyzes me.

I'm scared to death… of women.

Oh please, scoff not, as this is the genuine truth. I am absolutely terrified of women, and my fear, my dread, my terror goes back to my earliest memories. Allow me to continue to share this with you, so perhaps you may learn.

When I was four years old, still a year away from

being enrolled in the half-day kindergarten classes offered at Western Elementary School, it was my lot in life to join my mother in her weekly sojourn to the employer of my father. The company, a dairy plant, provided paychecks every Friday. My mother, concerned with our near-poverty existence and schedule of bills to be paid, chose to travel to the dairy plant each payday to get Dad's check rather than wait for him to bring it home and handle the financial deposits on another day. As reliable as the town clock tower, she always pulled into the parking lot near the docks where trucks delivered milk to the plant, and together, she and I awaited the appearance of Dad with his weekly check.

So, there it was, the weekly jaunt to the dairy plant.

On one particular Friday, my mother, who was heavily laden with the pregnancy which bore my younger sister, decided to park the car and visit the office staff at the dairy plant, as they had a gift for her in celebration of the upcoming birth. I was not particularly alarmed by this change of routine, and it allowed me to get out of the car and stretch my four-year-old legs a bit.

As we walked into the lobby, the receptionist directed Mom to the office on the left, where the ladies awaited her arrival. After a quick "Thank you!" Mom walked toward the office with me in tow. Then she stopped and gave me her purse to hold, and she walked into the room.

I stood in the doorway and looked into the large office space...

It was filled with women... and they were looking at me... and smiling...

I was terrified.

My mother motioned at me and said, "Come on! Come in here!"

But I couldn't move. I began to cry. And I refused to step into the room... that terrifying room... filled with women smiling at me...

To say such a frightening experience helped develop my phobia is but a disparage of the fact that I was emotionally damaged by the incident. Fear gripped me and held on.

When we returned to the safety and security of home, I ran back to my sister's room and dug out her copy of a Nancy Sinatra album. Till that day, I found the photo of Nancy to be overwhelmingly attractive. The cute blonde was tantalizing in her red and blue ensemble. But after that terrible experience at the dairy plant, I looked upon the photo with new eyes, and noticed by Nancy's stern look in the photo, she appeared to be angry with me, and based on the seriousness of her gaze, I was certain she wanted to beat me senseless. I put the album away, never again to gaze upon the lovely woman who wished to cause me harm.

As I grew older, I found myself more and more attracted to the female form.

When I started junior high school at the transitional age of thirteen, I discovered girls who had come from other elementary schools, and I gazed upon them with wonderment. They looked so pretty. I happily breathed in their perfumed fragrance after they walked by. I longed to touch their seemingly soft skin. I even made a list of the girls to whom I was most attracted, including girls who were in the grade above me.

Yet my fear kept me from pursuit of female affection for my entire seventh-grade year. I called no one my girlfriend and was without companionship. One day, the prettiest girl in the entire school, an eighth grader, spoke to me. Yes, she broke the girl/boy wall separating us and even spoke my name. Egads! She knew my identity! Her voice melodiously said my name, which caused me to break out in a sweat. I sat there, wondering if this was the moment for which I had hoped, and she was getting ready to ask me to marry her. Alas, she just asked a question pertaining to a contest being held at school. I could only nod my head. My normally active jaw muscles, paralyzed by her blinking doe-like eyes and the fact she knew my name, rendered me unable to speak. She never again breathed in my general direction.

Female teachers were not exempt from my affectionate longings, though I had enough sense to keep my thoughts to myself. However, there were three in particular to whom I would have gladly proposed had they been single and interested in a man who they could not legally marry for several years.

Near the middle of my eighth-grade year, I went for broke. One of those attractive, sweet girls appeared to like me, so I asked her to be my girlfriend. She accepted. Matrimonial joy overtook my fear, and the raging hormones, which rendered furry eruptions above my top lip and caused my vocal cords to skip octaves in the middle of a sentence, bid me to walk a bit more upright, with a hitherto unknown swagger in my step. I was inspired to poetry and wrote her several love sonnets, pledging my eternal devotion, or at least the best devotion I could muster at age fourteen.

Yet after a scant three weeks, she notified me our relationship must come to an end for undisclosed reasons. Destined was I to forevermore walk the earth alone, and the fear returned.

As I entered high school, the number of girls, plus the number of female teachers, increased exponentially. Again, I created a list of the girls I found most attractive, as they were most certainly the ones to fear. The female teachers, I again admired from a distance, even though I knew I was closer to the age to legally marry than I had been in junior high. This gave me hope.

By the time I was seventeen, I found myself in a relationship with a girl who had trapped me into a relationship by professing her attraction. Yes, she said she liked me.

I encountered great wrath from this girl at my every misstep, and I became aware that I much preferred debilitating fear and loneliness over the constant wrath from someone who professed such love and adoration yet enjoyed yelling at me. So, the relationship disintegrated, and my fear of women continued to grow.

In college, I found myself enrolled in a university where the male population outnumbered the women nearly ten to one. In such an environment, opportunities for love and affection were less than favorable, but some couples were noticed to spring up from time to time. One semester, I found myself within the clutches of Two-Month Mary, which I eventually called her, albeit behind her back, because she seemed to date everyone for two months. Before me, it was Richard, about whom I heard stories *every* time we were together. Their relationship lasted two months. Then Mary and I were together for two months. Then she moved on to my friend Stanley… for two months.

While we dated, Mary took great pleasure in telling me over and over, men tended to do everything wrong. Usually such a statement, followed by tales of all of Richard's errors, was shared immediately after a kiss. After listening to her tirade of the moment, which was typically filled with the same details I had heard in her manifesto from the previous day, I found it best to take her back home and bid her a good night.

Once, when I managed to kiss her and prevent the utterance of a repeat sermon, it appeared we might journey toward the hitherto unknown grounds of passionate lovemaking. Yet as we began to snuggle more intimately, she found it necessary to pull away and recite numerous statistics, most of which had to do with the number of women who found no pleasure in intimate settings.

Disgusted, I rose from the bed and turned on the light.

"Well! You certainly stopped in a hurry!" she huffed.

"Yeah. You just kinda spoiled the mood with your

timely sermon."

The evening ended very quietly, as she angrily refused to speak to me any further.

It had been two months.

I never got within twenty feet of her again – happily, I might add.

Many years later, when I found love and married, the intense fear of all women, including my spouse, continued to maintain its deathly grip upon my joy, squashing it beneath the sense of dread, and debilitating fear left me weak and senseless. She only tolerated me and never expressed in return the love I attempted to bestow upon her.

At one point in the marriage, she encountered several painful ailments requiring the attention of a physician specializing in the needs of the female of the species. Due to the intense occasional pain accompanying these afflictions, the physician insisted my ailing wife should not drive to the appointment, therefore I was designated to render assistance as her driver.

As we walked into the waiting room of the physician's office, I discovered to my horror, the facility, lined with chairs and couches of various degrees of comfort, was filled with women. Immediately the biblical story of Daniel in the lion's den, which was beaten into my head by my third-grade Sunday school teacher, came rushing back into my memory. As the eyes of the multitudes of women connected with mine, and the smell of a concentration of estrogen which must have exceeded all legal limits wafted into my nostrils, I became aware of the low, collective growl emanating from the souls of these women, in their hatred of my presence.

The fear, the extreme dread, the downright spooky feeling caused me to cower in a remote corner, seated upon some uncomfortable chair reserved for the hated and despised male of the species. Even though I was there out of kindness and concern for my wife, I was still a man, entirely unwelcome in this environment.

I prayed for deliverance.

Upon leaving the fearful office of the physician, I began once again to breathe and rejoiced in the fresh air outside the building.

Many years later, the marriage ended, and I found myself single again in my so-called middle age. The desire to have a fulfilling relationship with a woman was overpowered by the lifelong fear and dread, and I remained alone, safe.

At one point, a particularly attractive woman with whom I had the pleasure of acquaintance decided to marry a man from another state. This of course troubled me, as I was certain I should have been the man of this woman's dreams. Yet my standing as the man of her dreams was greatly hindered by the fact I was a mere acquaintance. She was far too attractive, and may I say a few years too young, for me to believe I could be of any interest. Therefore, I did not pursue requesting she accompany me for an evening of dining and conversation. That's right, I never asked her out.

She moved to the other state to be with the man of her choosing, yet I remained within her circle of acquaintances, and when announcement appeared of her temporary return for the sake of an engagement party, I marveled at being included on the list of invited individuals. The event, held at a local establishment similar to this one in which we now sit, promised to be an occasion of great joy, and I hoped to enjoy the company of various friends and acquaintances.

When I arrived at the specified den of libations, unfamiliarity with the building prevailed. Forced to enlist the help of an employee, I was directed to a room reserved for joyous occasions. I stopped at the door, peering nervously into the room, looking for the friendly face of any acquaintance.

There were none.

My eyes landed upon a long table, festooned with decorations of all kinds. In each chair around the long table was seated a young, attractive member of the female persuasion.

Yes, the room was filled with women.

They were busily engaged in conversations, complimenting each other's choice of clothing and accessories, or marveling at the pretty wrapped packages along the wall.

I took not another step into the room. I felt my face grow flush, and my heart began to race as I realized I was looking at a room not unlike the one my mother had forced me to see in my younger years. But rather than all the women being older than me as when I was four years old, this room was filled with women appearing to be younger than me. Knowledge of impending rejection stopped me in my tracks.

As I stood there, surveying the lovely feminine faces in hopes of finding someone I knew, my eyes met those of an attractive blonde who seemed to tower over the other ladies, even in a seated position. Yes, she was an amazon. My eyes locked in upon hers and within that fraction of a second, I could not look away.

Then the unspeakable happened…

She smiled at me.

Oh, the horror!

Oh, the agony!

Oh, the fear which swept over me as this woman, object of my greatest fear and trepidation, this beautiful spawn of Delilah herself, found me deserving of a smile.

In my panic, I managed to crack a smile in return, then without turning around, slowly and deliberately backed through the door, and hastily exited the establishment prior to the arrival of my acquaintance and the man of her choosing.

I tell you all these things, my friend and brother, so

you will understand my plight. A lifetime of fear of the female persuasion is of great *cripplance*.

Lastly, no doubt you are aware of the band which now adorns the third finger of my left hand. I am indeed once again bound by the vows of matrimony, to a lovely creature of the species, as lovely as any sister of Bathsheba might have dreamt of becoming. Her love for me astounds, and I marvel at the joy I find in this union.

To bring my elucidation to a close:

What astounds me, what confounds me, what I find worthy of great marvel, is the fact this beautiful, loving woman to whom I am betrothed doesn't scare me...

Or at least, not much... not yet...

CHASING SASQUATCH

———————— •●• ————————

B igfoot. Yep, we're going to go there.
That legendary tall hairy cryptid with a smelly disposition has been part of my bizarre life since 1975; November 1975, to be exact. One month before my eleventh birthday.

November 1975 saw the release of the movie *The Mysterious Monsters*, hosted by actor Peter Graves, of whom I was already a fan from his work on the television series *Mission: Impossible*. Now, here was that same guy, who in my head he was still his M.I. character Jim Phelps, telling stories about several sightings of monsters, including the abominable snowman, the Loch Ness Monster, and Bigfoot, in a movie shown in theaters. The previews on television scared the bejeebers out of me, especially one part where it showed the creature walking past a window, the shadow of which appeared on the drawn curtain, and then suddenly a big hairy arm smashes through the glass and almost grabs the screaming lady on the couch.

However, the most important part of the previews was the Roger Patterson footage. This was real, honest to goodness filmed evidence of the existence of this massive hairy beast, and this time, it was a girl monster! The now famous but jumpy, out-of-focus footage showed a female Bigfoot creature walking away slowly, with arms and breasts swaying, then turning to look back at the camera. It was spellbinding, I tell ya, spellbinding!

I wanted to go see the movie; but then again, I didn't want to go see the movie. I was fascinated and terrified.

Somewhere deep down inside, I realized once I saw this film, I would never sleep again. In the end, I didn't see it before its departure from the theater in town. But that cryptid-infatuated boy was forever converted to the Church of Bigfoot.

The summer of 1976 was a turning point in my growing obsession with the monster. Nearly every summer, my family traveled to Kansas City, Missouri, to spend a few days with my mother's maternal aunt, Alice Jarman. She had a wonderful old two-story house with a full basement, lots of corners and crevices for playing, and pretty little bedrooms upstairs. It was a terrific place for a kid to spend time, and my great aunt was a lovely, fun lady.

That summer, true to form, the whole gang packed up and went to Alice's house for a few days. One night, Dad was watching the ten o'clock news in the front room, and my brother and I were watching along, since we looked forward to staying up late and switching through the local programming after the news. During the news broadcast, a story came up about a sighting of a creature called Mo-Mo. I had never heard of Mo-Mo, so my ears perked up to listen. According to the news anchor, throughout history, Bigfoot-type creatures have been sighted in every state of the Union, and Mo-Mo was the name attributed to Bigfoot sightings within our state. Work with me on this: Mo-Mo stands for Missouri Monster.

My eleven-year-old mind blew a gasket.

What? Bigfoot/Mo-Mo/whatever has been sighted in Missouri? You mean he doesn't just live in Colorado or Washington or Oregon?

I didn't sleep very well through the night. I lay in bed in one of the upstairs rooms, scared to death I was going to look out into the dark hallway and see the shadow of Mo-Mo stalking up the stairs to get me. Of course, in the terror of that night, it did not occur to me the chances of a Bigfoot creature inhabiting a heavily populated neighborhood in metropolitan Kansas City were very slim. All I could think of was he/she/it was out there, waiting for me.

Afterward, knowing there were Bigfoot monsters in Missouri, eleven-year-old Tim began to worry about the occasional trips taken to the lovely town of Shell Knob, Missouri, on the shores of Table Rock Lake, where my maternal grandfather Earl Moore lived in a mobile home park called Lakeview Acres. Grandpa, an avid fisherman, had occupied the same location since long before I was born. The park was situated upon a high spot in the area from which you could see the lake from several locations, thus the name Lakeview Acres. In my mind, it should have also been called "Bigfoot-Probably-Lives-Nearby Acres," as it was nestled within the Mark Twain National Forest, and the window in my grandmother's bedroom, which served as a guest bedroom when she wasn't there, looked right out into the deep, dark pine forest I knew must harbor the furry giant.

At the age of eleven, I didn't have to worry quite as much about lying in Grandma's bed and having a Bigfoot break the window and reach in to grab me. At that age, Mom and Dad slept in the back bedroom, and my brother, younger sister, and I crammed ourselves into the hide-a-bed couch in the living room. So instead of worrying about being grabbed in the back bedroom, I worried about a Bigfoot walking between trailers in the park, seeing us sleeping on the hide-a-bed in front of the big window there in the living room, and then of course smashing the window and trying to grab us. I typically refused to sleep closest to the window, though I did not divulge my reasons.

Back home, one day we went to the public library in town, and I found a book about Bigfoot, and it was the only book I checked out that day. I read it from cover to cover, and then over again. I learned about how Native Americans had long told stories about Sasquatch, their name for a giant hairy human living in the forest. I learned about

Albert Ostman, who claimed in 1924 in the forests of British Columbia he was kidnapped and held captive by a family of Bigfoot – or should it be Bigfeet? – until he escaped. I was mesmerized.

At some point during that summer, I decided the next logical step in my obsession with the cryptid was to incorporate Bigfoot into my writing. Up to that point, my writing career, which began at the age of eight, had included three poems and a series of plays which I performed for my schoolmates, which subsequently caused my lovely female teacher to begin balding at an early age. But in 1975, with visions of Sasquatch filling my thoughts, I embarked on the creation of my first novel. It was an adventure story about a boy, Tommy Cummingsworth, who just happened to be about my age. He was smart, ornery, and adventurous, and I decided to call my book *The Mischievous Little Boy*, which I later updated to call *The Mischievous Kid*, since in my continuing maturity, I decided "Little Boy" sounded entirely too childish. The book already had four stunning chapters, each one about four pages long, including illustrations by my artistic brother, but that summer, I decided the book needed a chapter about the monster. Hence the chapter called "Tommy Meets Bigfoot" was created within a timespan of about thirty minutes.

Before going any further, I feel I should mention there is only one copy of *The Mischievous Little Boy/Kid* in existence. Written and illustrated by hand in pencil on notebook paper and stapled together, the reader can breathe a sigh of relief to know this spectacular volume of literary genius will never see the light of day.

However, for the reader's enjoyment, I wish to present in its entirety, minus illustrations, Chapter Five: Tommy Meets Bigfoot:

There he was. Tommy Cummingsworth was in Colorado. His family had been planning this trip for weeks!

Tommy looked out his log cabin window. The sun was bright in his eyes and – wait! Something is out there. He looked. His mouth dropped open. It was Bigfoot, the mysterious monster that had been unknown to man for years. Tommy ran out to try to catch him, but he couldn't. Bigfoot was seven feet tall.

Tommy caught up with the monster. He jumped onto Bigfoot's back. The monster threw him off.

The next day, Tommy woke up in a hospital bed. He had ruptured his back. The cause: Bigfoot's throw! He had to stay in the hospital for two more days. When he got out, he ran into the woods to find Bigfoot. He saw him sitting on a rock. Bigfoot saw him and ducked, for fear Tommy would beat him. Tommy sat down and comforted the monster.

Tommy heard his mother calling. He said goodbye to the monster and went home. The next day, Tommy went to see the monster. Bigfoot took Tommy to his cave where he had a family. They had fun and played games. But Tommy had to leave and go back home to Chicago. He left and waved goodbye.

A stunning bit of prose, if I do say so myself.

With my Pulitzer Prize almost guaranteed, I considered myself to be not only a gifted writer but also one of the premiere experts on the subject of Bigfoot and set out to do all I could to spread the word and ensure the creature's existence would be proven.

Around the same time, I spent hours perfecting my masterful piece of literature, two science fiction shows dominated television viewing: *The Six Million Dollar Man* and its spinoff, *The Bionic Woman*. Both of these early versions of cyborgs were a favorite in my childhood household, and along with my siblings, I was glued to my chair in the living room when either show was on. As happened often in 1970s television, programs would have a two- or three-part storyline. Just when the story appeared to reach a climax, the words "Continued Next Episode" appeared, drawing a collective moan from everyone in the room.

In February of 1976, such an episode appeared on *The Six Million Dollar Man* which piqued my interest. It was called "The Secret of Bigfoot, Part One." I was ecstatic! At last, here was a nationally televised show featuring Bigfoot, and would no doubt accomplish several things. First, it would show people what the monster really looked like, since hitherto the only photographs were blurry. Second, it would accurately show people the cryptid was a harmless animal who needed to be understood. Third, it would portray Bigfoot in such a truthful and factual manner so no one would be doubtful of its existence. I secretly wished they would have asked me to be a consultant for the show, as I could have taught them so much from my vast knowledge. Plus, it would have no doubt afforded me close contact with the lead female guest star on the episode, Stefanie Powers, in whom my pre-pubescent mind was highly interested.

In the opening scenes of the show, viewers learned two friends of the lead character, Steve Austin, the aforementioned Six Million Dollar Man, disappeared in the California wilderness, and upon discovery of a large footprint, the presence of a Bigfoot was suspected, and the lead characters immediately jumped to the conclusion the cryptid had caused it, implying possible foul play.

I was mortified to see the writers of the show making such accusations but endeavored to continue watching in hopes my smelly, furry hero would be vindicated.

Alas, the show progressed and eventually Steve Austin came face-to-face with Bigfoot. Finally, the world got to see the true appearance of the beast. The two fought each other, and it was an intense scene filled with slow motion 70s-era action. Then suddenly Steve Austin ripped the beast's arm off. Sparks flew, and viewers were led to believe Bigfoot wasn't a true animal; he was a machine!

How dare they? I was offended and so very disillusioned. These people were not interested in telling the truth about Bigfoot. They were making stuff up! Why would they do that?

I still watched as the plot twisted and turned, revealing Bigfoot was bionic himself, and associated with aliens who had set up shop in a cave in the mountains of California, protected by a rotating ice tunnel which made you pass out and lose your memory. I wondered why I couldn't write stuff of this quality. Steve was taken into the cave, where I got my first glimpse of Stefanie Powers and thoroughly enjoyed any scene in which she appeared in the episode, as well as within Part Two.

After the airing of the episode, all of my friends who liked the show were talking about it at school, spouting incorrect notions about Bigfoot. I decided I needed to take control of the situation and become the authoritative voice in all things related to the beast, for the school, the city, the state, and eventually the entire world. It was then and there, I created the Bigfoot Investigations Agency, or BIA for short, of which I was the president.

The goals of the BIA were numerous. We first and foremost were tasked with educating the public about our smelly fuzzy friend. Second, it was our duty to investigate firsthand any reported sightings in the neighborhood and around the school. Thirdly, we were to organize ourselves so if any sightings occurred within the state, we were to go there, camp, and investigate to see if we could find and make contact with the beast, documenting everything with photographs which were not blurry like all the others known to the public. We were pretty much to be a team of Sasquatch Minutemen. Lastly, we were to serve as a research society, studying past photographs and amassing a large library of information.

Somehow, I learned there was a Bigfoot research center in The Dalles, Oregon, headed up by a man by the name of Peter Bryne. He was featured in the movie *The Mysterious Monsters*, so I decided to offer him the assistance of the BIA. Being a consummate packrat, I had saved a photo of Bigfoot, which was a still from the Patterson footage, and decided my first task should be to examine the photograph under a magnifying glass, to see if I could provide a clearer image of the beast. I grabbed a piece of paper and began to draw my interpretation of Bigfoot's face as well as the body, knowing this would be of great assistance to Mr. Bryne. I wrote him a letter, telling him who I was and the mission of the BIA, and included the drawing, saying I hoped it would help with his research. I also asked if there were any books, posters, T-shirts, or anything else available to further announce to the world that I was an expert.

Several weeks went by, then one day, a large envelope arrived from Oregon. I was thrilled and ran to my room to read the expected letter of thanks from Mr. Bryne, and whatever else he included. Deep down inside, I expected to receive an offer to move there and become one of the researchers on his staff. I didn't realize until many years later the Bigfoot Research Center was operated out of an old trailer and had no staff.

Inside the envelope were several pages of many different colors which appeared to be photocopies of pages which had been replicated several times before, nearly as fuzzy as most photographs of Bigfoot. They included information about posters, T-shirts, and books, all of which were more expensive than my unemployed, nonexistent bank account could afford. But the real gold mine was the Bigfoot Fact Sheet. It was filled with a multitude of details, most of which I already knew.

I gathered up the priceless documentation from the world-renowned Bigfoot Research Center and decided I needed to have a folder to contain the precious material for training, which no doubt would occur as throngs of people would flock toward me to learn more about Sasquatch. So, I took two pieces of thin cardboard and stapled them together on three sides. Then I grabbed that photograph I had of the still from the Patterson footage and glued it to the front. Then next to the photo, in black magic marker, I wrote in big letters "Bigfoot Investigations Agency" and God only knows what else. I stuffed the pages from the BRC into my newly created corporate dossier, created some hand-lettered business cards with a big footprint on them and in bold magic marker letters "Bigfoot Investigations Agency" and my name below with my position "President and Lead Investigator," and took the folder and cards to school with me every day, to show my sasquatch-enthusiast buddies.

One of my friends, an odd kid by the name of Jay, who many years later found fame as a convicted murderer, asked if he could borrow the folder to look at the papers more closely. I foolishly said yes, and when he returned it, he said, "I took the liberty of assigning security clearances to all these documents."

"You did what?" I asked, a bit puzzled over the necessity of security clearances.

"Oh of course." He was very matter-of-fact about all of it. "Only certain people need to see the items with the highest security clearance."

I looked at the sheets. On some, he had written "Top Secret." On others, he wrote "More Top Secret," then on one or two he wrote "Toppest Secret."

I made sure I never let him borrow the folder unattended again.

In August of 1976, I began sixth grade, a ripe old man in my last year of elementary school. September typically ushered in the new season of television shows, and to my excitement, *The Six Million Dollar Man* and *The Bionic Woman* aired a two-part series called "The Return of Bigfoot." I quickly forgot how appalled I had been earlier in the year with the show and their portrayal of Sasquatch as a bionic being from outer space. It probably had something to do with my enjoyment of watching Stefanie Powers on the show. I was prepared this time to just scoff at their audacity to portray the beast in such a way and settled in to enjoy watching Ms. Powers again as well as the Bionic Woman's star Lindsey Wagner. I had always been a bit girl crazy, but fastly approaching the manly age of twelve, it kicked into overdrive.

The show did not disappoint on two fronts: Bigfoot was handled poorly, and the ladies were fun to watch.

Motivated by the two episodes highlighting Bigfoot on national television, I decided to write my next book. This one was going to be about an ordinary guy who became a great crime fighter then Bigfoot hunter. I called the book *Radarman*, not because it had anything to do with the flimsy plot I had cooked up in my mind; I just thought it sounded cool.

The book got off to a rocky start when I killed off my main character after four pages. Undeterred, I continued on, and the story developed into a powerful page-turner, filled with action and intrigue which can only come from the fertile mind of a twelve-year-old. When my surviving character decided to turn from crime fighter to Bigfoot investigator, the words flowed easily from pencil to paper due to my own experiences as a seasoned investigator. In the end, I took the humane route in handling the beast, as my character wanted to keep his Bigfoot captive, yet realized he needed to be in the wild, and ultimately set him free.

As my sixth-grade year progressed, and 1976 turned into 1977, I began to ponder the next steps for the Bigfoot Investigations Agency. I had not yet achieved Man of the World status. I hadn't really made it to Man of Missouri status either. Hell, I was barely a Man of Westport Elementary. I began to realize when I moved to the next step in my education, which was to be at Harry P. Study Junior High School, I would meet new people – including more girls. Additionally, it occurred to me, I might actually want to have a girlfriend someday; not the childish boyfriend/girlfriend stuff of elementary school but rather the committed adult relationship experience which can only happen when you are a mature and wise thirteen-year-old. What would the female population of Study Junior High think of my status as president and lead investigator in the BIA? Would they be impressed with my hand made business cards? Would they flock to me, surround me and adore me, all the while begging me to show them the Patterson footage?

By the time sixth grade ended, and the harsh reality set in that I was moving up in the world, I took a long look into the mirror and decided I needed to disband the Bigfoot Investigations Agency. I took stock of our accomplishments:

Number of trips to investigate Bigfoot sightings: Zero.

Number of seminars held to educate the masses about cryptids: Zero.

Number of members: Two, including my eight-year-old sister, a devoted follower.

Number of organizational meetings: Zero.

Sheets of paper with security clearances scribbled on them: Six.

I felt like it was time to let the BIA fade into the sunset. I stuffed my folder full of information into the packrat box of junk under my bed and walked away from it.

When I started junior high, I felt like a new man. I made new friends, got some new clothes before school started, and even combed my hair differently, parted in the middle instead of to one side. I tucked my books about The Mischievous Boy and Radarman safely into that box under my bed where no one would find them, and said nothing about Bigfoot to anyone, hoping my friends from sixth grade would forget all about it. Two years later, as eighth grade was coming to an end and I was looking forward to yet another new start in high school, one of the girls with whom I had been friends in sixth grade brought it up. At that moment, I wanted to perform some sort of Stefanie Powers memory cancellation spell on her, hoping she might wake up with no recollection on our first day of high school. My friend's memory notwithstanding, I skated through high school and college with no further reminders of my cryptid-obsessed past. In my adult life, I have written and published other compositions, staying safely away from any mention of Bigfoot – until now.

I've said those two earliest books I wrote in elementary school went to hell when I brought Sasquatch into them. Now, here I am, adding a story about the beast to my latest book.

Will I ever learn?

About the Author

Photo by Erin Northrip, Gambles Photography

A native of Springfield, Missouri, Tim Ritter grew up in a performing family and discovered writing and public speaking early in life. By age 13, his writings included poetry, two children's adventure books, several plays, and a comic strip which eventually found its way to his junior high school newspaper. He also discovered that he liked being on stage, and how people tended to listen when he spoke into a microphone.

Throughout his 29-year professional career as a mechanical engineer, Tim wrote articles for trade magazines and was the featured speaker at hundreds of seminars across the country.

Tim lives outside Fair Grove, Missouri, with his wife, Lisa, writing full-time and speaking to civic groups and organizations on a variety of topics. In addition to being past president of the Springfield Writers Guild, he is a member of Sleuth's Ink Mystery Writers, the historical societies in Douglas and Christian Counties, Ozarks Genealogical Society, and the Poe Studies Association.

OTHER BOOKS BY TIM RITTER

Sarah and Orville, released in 2024, is a prequel to *Sarah Burning*, providing the backstory and family histories of Sarah Ritter and her husband Orville. Also included in the book is additional information that surfaced after publication of *Sarah Burning*, including six letters that she wrote to her twin sons in the months leading up to The Fire, as well as stills from video footage of the house and family that was also discovered after the publication of the 2021 book.

Tim's award-winning *Sarah Burning*, released in 2021, tells the true story of a fatal housefire in rural Missouri in 1959, and the struggle of the three survivors who had to put the physical and emotional pain, survivor guilt, and horrifying memories of that night behind them. It is a story of perseverance, strength, and redemption in which everyone, including the rest of the family, had to literally rise from the ashes.

Soul Sketches – 2ⁿᵈ Edition, released in 2020, is a heartfelt collection of short stories and poems, most of which are based on Tim's personal experiences. He refers to the book as a "real, sometimes brutal, look at life, death, marriage, divorce, and everything in between."